D

A Romany Story
William Lee

Bill Lee

Dark Blood

A Romany Story

William Lee

First Published 1999 by
MINERVA PRESS
315-317 Regent Street
London
W1R 7YB

Acknowledgement

I would like to take this opportunity to thank my daughter Shelley whom without her writing skills my story would not have been written on paper as I myself could only dictate it.

And to my wife, for believing in me and giving me the confidence to tell this story.

And to thank the reader I hope you enjoy it.

This is a novel based upon oral history as related by Bill Lee from his own experience and tales handed down to him. Several names and places have been altered. No offence is intended in relating these stories of human encounters and deeply founded prejudices, which are often violently expressed.

Chapter One
The Letter – 1940

The weather had grown hot and Bill could feel every one of the sun's burning rays on his tired back. Still, it would not be long, if his guess was right, before he would be able to go home for dinner.

'Home,' he said, and laughed out loud.

Home was a tiny wagon drawn by a horse, but it didn't matter however small the wagon was; when he had finished a long hard working day, he could go home to see his wife Naomi and his small son, Ethan. His wagon felt like a mansion and he felt like a king. Naomi, he thought. She was a beautiful Gypsy woman with long chestnut hair and mysterious dark eyes. She had a pencil-slim figure and hands that showed she had worked hard in her twenty-five years. He loved her just as much now as on the day he had married her.

'Bill!' a voice called, making him jump and snapping him out of his daydreams. 'Time for dinner,' shouted the young man, who was called John. 'And there's a letter for you up at the farm.'

'Thanks,' Bill said, bending to pick up his bag and flinging it over his shoulder. He left the hop field, walking with an easy grace. He was a tall man, with a strong muscular build that reflected a life of hard labouring. He had ruggedly handsome features and short dark curly hair, but instead of having the dark eyes, which usually accompanied such dark hair and skin, his eyes were stunningly blue.

'Afternoon, Bill,' said Frank Reeves, the farmer who owned the farm where Bill worked.

'Afternoon, sir,' Bill replied. 'I hear you have a letter for me.

'That's right, sonny,' the old man said. 'Arrived this morning, it did, and I don't think it's the bearer of good news. Half the other lads working here have got one, too.'

'Would you mind reading my letter for me?' Bill asked. 'Only, as you know, I can't read or write myself.'

'Of course not,' said the old man, opening the letter. 'I'm afraid it's bad news, Bill. You've got your call up papers. And you've only got two weeks before you start your training. Looks like the war gets to us all in the end. Good luck, son,' he said, giving Bill back his letter and striding away.

'Wait!' Bill called. 'Would you mind if I took the rest of the day off work, so I won't have to leave Naomi when I tell her the news?'

'Of course not,' the old man replied and walked away.

Bill stood stock-still in the middle of the courtyard, staring ahead of him. This was going to be the hardest thing he was ever going to have to do, he thought, turning the letter over and over in his hands. It was just a piece of paper to him. He couldn't read any of it, and yet these very words would change his life forever.

Still, he had to tell Naomi, he thought, turning and walking in the direction of the wagon, back through the same apple orchard he had gone through that morning; but now he failed to notice the beauty of the blossom or the lovely scent. His mind was on one thing, to tell

Naomi and to spend as much of the next two weeks as he could with her and Ethan.

He walked on to the field where the wagon was pulled up. He found Naomi bending over the tub doing their washing and little Ethan playing.

'Ethan,' he called. The small boy ran excitedly towards his father, to be thrown into the air and caught in a pair of strong hands. Giggling, he threw his arms tightly around his father's neck and planted a sticky kiss on his cheek.

Naomi looked up to see her husband striding towards her with their son in his arms. How alike father and son were; but it was her dark eyes the boy had inherited. Then she looked at Bill. She could tell at once that something was wrong, and Bill had a letter in his hand, a letter he was now handing to her. She'd had some schooling years ago, and was able to read the letter, but before she reached the last line her vision was blurred with tears. Her Bill had to go and fight in the war. Naomi crumpled the letter into a ball and threw it away.

'Don't cry, Naomi,' Bill said softly, 'everything will be fine.'

Naomi looked at him, her cheeks reddening in anger. You're not seriously thinking about going and fighting that war, are you?' she said sharply. 'What has this country ever given you? Nothing! Absolutely nothing! You've had to work and fight for everything you've got, and this country hasn't helped us one little bit – and now they want you to go and fight! Well, to hell with all of it!' She exclaimed. We'll run away somewhere where they won't find us.'

'No,' Bill said, stopping her angry outburst. 'You may think I haven't got anything to fight for, but I have. I've got a wife and a son, and I'll go and I'll fight for your freedom as well as my own. My father didn't run, and neither shall I.'

The next two weeks Bill and Naomi spent their time as if it was their very last together – and hoping it was not. All too soon came the time when Bill had to leave for his training. Holding Naomi and Ethan tight, standing on the railway platform, Bill promised he would be back to see them both before he sailed to fight in the war.

Naomi stayed on the farm working for Mr Reeves. Training the hop-bines was hard work but it paid her and Ethan's way, and kept her mind occupied. Only at night when Ethan was asleep did she feel the loneliness surrounding her. Now that Bill was gone she missed him and couldn't wait to see him again. Having no family she had nobody else to turn to.

✳ ✳ ✳

Some weeks later Naomi stepped out of her wagon. It was a lovely day and the sun was shining out of a clear blue sky. Hop training had finished the week before and she was resting until cherry picking started. Sitting on the steps to the wagon her head resting in her hands, deep in thought, with her chestnut hair hanging free to her waist, she made a beautiful sight. Mr Reeves had let Naomi and Ethan stay in his field, and for this she was grateful; but sooner or later she would have to move on and start cherry picking. Naomi glanced up. In the distance she could see a figure walking towards the wagon.

Thinking it could be anybody, Naomi got up and started to go into the wagon when she heard her name being called. Looking around, Naomi could now see clearly who the man was; it was Bill. He had kept his promise to come home and see them, even if it was only for a little while. Walking the short distance that separated them, Naomi put her arms around her man in khaki and held him tight. How good it felt to have him near, to be held in his arms. Naomi felt much more alive than she had done for weeks.

Naomi and Bill talked for what seemed like hours. They played with Ethan until the child fell asleep, exhausted. Bill told Naomi that he could only stay three days but that in these three days, he would not leave her side. Then the night was theirs alone. Lying in Bill's arms, listening to the sound of his breathing as he slept, Naomi longed for the days to go slowly. How she loved and wanted Bill by her side for always, but she knew at the same time that this could not be. He had to go to war and she had to accept this. With these thoughts in her mind Naomi fell into a fitful sleep.

All too soon the days went by and Bill had to leave.

'You look so handsome in your uniform,' Naomi told him, as he looked at her with his piercing blue eyes, his wavy hair cut so short. Naomi reached out a hand and touched his hair. 'I love you,' she told him.

'And I love you,' Bill replied, bending to kiss her gently.

He would miss them, but as he held them close he knew it was for their freedom that he must go and fight.

Letting Naomi and Ethan go, Bill looked at Naomi. 'Don't cry,' he said, gently brushing the tears from her face, with the back of his hand. 'Before you know it, I'll be home again.' Then, picking up his bag and, saying goodbye, he started to walk away.

'Wait,' Naomi called, 'I'll walk with you to the courtyard.'

Walking through the green fields and apple orchards with Ethan trotting along on one side of her and Bill striding out on the other, Naomi tried not to think that Bill was leaving. She made herself forget for a while and enjoyed those precious moments. Then they reached the courtyard. Here they had to say goodbye. Holding Ethan in her arms and watching Bill walk away into the distance, Naomi thought of her promise to travel down and see Bill off at Dover docks.

She would see him one more time before he left, she thought, but that didn't ease the pain of seeing him walk away from her now. Tears blurred her vision again and spilled down onto her cheeks. Just before Bill turned the corner at the top of the courtyard, he turned back to look at Naomi and Ethan, and waved. Seeing his father waving goodbye, Ethan waved his chubby hand and shouted, 'Goodbye.'

Naomi waved too, until Bill was out of sight. When Bill was gone Naomi looked at Ethan: 'Let's go home, Ethan,' she said.

Chapter Two
Jack and Martha

'It looks like it's just the two of us again,' said Naomi as she made her way back to the wagon; but she knew she could not stay there much longer. When she put Ethan to bed that night, Naomi felt the familiar feeling of loneliness return. She prayed to God that is would not always be this way.

Naomi received word three days later that Bill would soon be embarking. With this in mind, she started her journey to Dover docks to see Bill off. She told Mr Reeves that she had to leave.

'That's all right,' he said, 'all your work's finished here, anyway, for this time of the year. I didn't want to tell you, but the council's been on to me for some time now because they say that the caravan's been parked in the field too long.'

'I'm sorry about that, Mr Reeves,' said Naomi.

'Oh, think nothing of it,' he replied, and tell Bill I wish him well.

With these words echoing in her head, Naomi began her journey.

* * *

'Come on Martha,' Jack Bray called to his sister. 'I've been sitting here for ages. We'll never get there on time.'

'You shouldn't be in such a hurry,' Martha said, as she came bustling through the front door of their house.

'How does my hat look?' she asked, holding it on top of her head with one hand while trying to pull herself up into the cart with the other.

'Fine,' Jack said, 'you look just fine, Martha.'

When Martha was settled on the cart, Jack nudged the horse and started it moving.

＊ ＊ ＊

'Jack,' Martha said, turning to look at him, 'why did we have to accept the invitation from the manor?'

'Because, Martha, we earn a good living from the manor, and the Squire's a fine gentleman. It seemed only right we accept their invitation to dinner. It's only once a year, after all.'

Martha turned back, and looked solemnly at the road. The next few miles were spent in companionable silence, while Martha thought of the many times she had travelled that way to Jack's farm and smithy with her late husband to visit her lonesome brother. Jack thought the silence was unusual for Martha, who was generally never short of a few things to say. Suddenly she asked, 'Jack, how much further do we have to go?'

Jack rolled his eyes heavenward. He knew the silence could not have lasted. 'Quite a way, and I bet we'll be late,' he told her.

'Oh, Jack!' Martha exclaimed, 'you've got your old boots on. Why didn't you wear the new ones I bought you?'

'Because these are much more comfortable,' he said, 'and I've cleaned them up. Anyway, no one will be looking at my boots!'

In the distance they heard the humming of an aeroplane engine.

'Sounds like a fighter,' Jack said.

'I hope it's not a German,' Martha said. 'Let's sit awhile in the trees. They cover the road, so we won't be seen.'

Jack saw the plane climbing high in the sky. It was a German ME 109. It climbed into the clouds and disappeared.

'I don't think he's coming back,' Jack said, and they pulled towards the crossroads. They saw a half-mile marker to the manor, as they rounded the bend, and then Jack pulled up short. 'What on earth's that?' he exclaimed. 'It looks like a Gypsy caravan; but what's it doing lying on its side in the ditch like that?'

'Look,' cried Martha, 'the poor horse is down as well!'

Jack jumped down from the trap. I'll take a look and see if there is anyone around.' Jack could not find anyone in the caravan. Suddenly he cried, 'Martha come and have a look at this!'

Martha climbed down for a closer inspection. 'It looks like it's been shot up,' she said. 'There're bullet holes all over it.'

'And the horse is dead!' said Jack, leaning over the still animal.

'I bet it was that German plane,' said Martha, shaking a fist at the sky.

'Listen!' Jack hushed her. 'Can you hear somebody crying?'

Jack walked back to the ditch and peered into the bushes. He could see a young woman cuddling a child, hiding in fear. 'Over here!' he called.

Martha came hurrying over. 'Oh my poor dears, are you from the caravan?' she asked.

'Yes,' answered the young woman, 'it was the plane! It machined-gunned our wagon. Now what am I going to do?' she cried in dismay.

'Give me your hand,' said Jack, 'I'll help you up.'

'Take my little boy first,' she said, handing Jack her small son.

He lifted the boy and then went back for the woman. She weighed next to nothing, he thought, and she was very thin. Naomi sat on the bank and pulled Ethan into her arms. There she rocked him, and cried. Martha sat beside her and tried to comfort her.

'There now, my dear,' she said and gently asked,

'Where is your husband?'

The small boy lifted his head from his mother's shoulder and looked at Martha. 'Daddy's in Heaven,' he said his big brown eyes filling with tears, 'there's only me and Mummy.'

'We were trying to find somewhere to stop when that aeroplane came,' said his mother.

Martha looked at Jack. 'We can't leave them here,' she said. 'We have to do something. You say what you like, Jack but they need somewhere to stay for a while and they both need to rest.'

'What are you thinking of?' asked Jack.

'We've got to take them in with us,' Martha replied.

'We cannot leave them here!'

Jack took what he could from the wagon and promised Naomi that he would be back with a team of horses that could pull the wagon out of the ditch. He told her he was very sorry, but he could do nothing about the horse; it was dead. Naomi bowed her head. Her world was falling apart.

It was decided that Martha would take Naomi and Ethan home with the horse and cart, leaving Jack to walk the rest of the way to the manor. 'I'll tell them you're not well,' he said 'or think up some excuse.'

Martha turned the cart around to take the young lady and her child home, and Jack went in the direction of the manor.

Naomi did not say a word all the way back to Tattlebury Smithy and Martha thought it was best to leave her, for she seemed to be in a world of her own. They finally reached the house. Martha took Naomi and Ethan inside and they were soon sitting around the kitchen table. Neither of them had spoken a word. They seemed to be in a state of shock.

Martha lit the lanterns and the fire and made a cup of tea. 'Drink this, my dear, it will make you feel better,' she said.

'Thank you,' said Naomi, taking the cup in her two hands, drinking some of the warm comforting tea.

Martha turned to the lad. 'What is your name, young man' she asked.

Ethan,' the small boy replied, 'and my mummy's name is Naomi.'

'And my name is Martha,' she said smiling. 'Are you hungry, Ethan? Would you like some dinner or some cake?'

Ethan wanted some cake, but Naomi refused. She drank tea but ate nothing. Martha told them that she would make up beds for them.

While Martha was out of the kitchen, Naomi looked around. There were wooden cupboards and a window above the sink with plain linen curtains. In the corner was a range; it was nothing like her Queenie stove in her wagon. She had to smile to herself – she would be able to fit the whole of her wagon in this kitchen. Just then Martha returned and said she would show them to their rooms. Martha showed Naomi to one room and Ethan to another.

'I want to stay with mummy,' the young boy said to Martha, looking around him with wide frightened eyes.

'How old are you, Ethan?' Martha asked.

'He's five,' Naomi replied, as she walked through the bedroom door.

'I thought he was older,' Martha said.

'He's been through a lot already in his young life,' Naomi said. 'That's why he seems older than he is. He can stay in my room with me. He doesn't like being on his own.'

Martha saw that they were settled and then left them to sleep. All through the night she worried constantly and checked her guests, but they slept soundly. It was early next morning before Martha saw her brother again, when Jack arrived home with the wagon.

He must have come back in the night to collect the horses and gone back again. Thinking about it, Martha didn't remember hearing Jack come into the house at all.

Seeing Martha standing at the kitchen window, Jack called to her, waving his hand to attract her attention.

Martha went out into the yard. 'What's the matter, Jack?' she asked.

'Could I have something to eat and a drink, Martha,' asked Jack, 'only it's taken me ages! I've worked all through the night, and I'm staving.

'Come into the kitchen,' Martha replied, 'and I'll cook you something.'

'Not now,' said Jack with a rather determined look on his face. 'Let me get this caravan out of sight first.'

'But Jack,' Martha pleaded, 'you're exhausted! And what are you going to do with it anyway?'

'I'm going to put it in that old barn that we don't use,' he said.

'Jack, it's falling down,' Martha argued.

'It will do for a while until I can get something else sorted out,' Jack retorted, 'Now help me, Martha I'm too exhausted to do it alone.'

When the wagon was pulled into the barn and safely under lock and key, Jack and Martha made their way back to the house.

'Did you go to the manor?' Martha asked Jack as they went in through the front door.

'Yes, I got there,' Jack replied. 'I told them that you were unwell and that I had to return home straight away. They were quite understanding.' He yawned and gave a tired sigh. 'Now that the wagon is out of sight, I must dispose of the horse,' he went on, almost as if he was talking to himself.

Martha made sure that Jack was seated at the kitchen table with a hot cup of tea before she began to cook his breakfast. As she cracked two eggs into the frying pan, the kitchen door swung open and Naomi and Ethan stepped into the room.

'I'm grateful for all you've done,' said Naomi, 'but we have to be going now. Winter will soon be upon us, and I have to make it to the New Forest to prepare for the cold months.'

There was a short silence. Martha looked at Jack and then back to Naomi. 'But child,' Martha said, 'you can't go. Your wagon is badly damaged and you would never survive the journey on foot. Besides, what would you do for money?'

Naomi looked at Martha's kind face, her twinkling blue eyes and the blonde hair newly touched with white. Her slight figure, small mouth and a dainty nose were set in a heart-shaped face. Yes, thought Naomi, this is the face of someone who really cares.

'You don't have to worry,' Naomi said. 'I have money and I have gold. Believe me, money is the last of my worries.'

Jack left the kitchen table and went towards Naomi. 'Jack Bray,' he said holding out his hand, 'and your name is Naomi, if I'm not mistaken.'

She smiled at him and held out her hand. 'That's right,' she said.

'You know, young lady,' he said, 'you're more than welcome to stay for a few more days. I'm a blacksmith and I can repair your wagon for you. And, as you have gold and money, I can buy you another horse! Then you can be on your way.'

'What do you say?' asked Martha. 'Will you stay?'

Naomi smiled at them both. 'Yes,' she replied, 'I will stay a few more days.'

'Good!' laughed Martha. 'Now, come on everyone, I'll make you all some breakfast.'

'She's in her element now!' Jack said, nodding his head towards Martha and pulling a funny face that made Ethan giggle.

Martha pulled all the blinds down on the windows for the blackout and asked Jack to light the lanterns. She would cook breakfast for all of them, and it would be the earliest breakfast they were ever going to have.

Jack finished his breakfast first, saying that he had to go on his way now to deal with the horse. He told them he would see them later and left the house.

Martha looked at Ethan and Naomi sitting at the kitchen table and asked, 'Where do you come from? How far have you travelled?'

For a moment there was silence, and then Naomi took a deep breath. 'Where do I begin?' she said with a sigh. 'We were staying at Peasmarsh on Leigh Farm, not far from Rye. We were working for a man called Mr Frank Reeves. Bill, my husband, went to work one Tuesday morning as usual and that dinnertime Mr Reeves came and told him there was a letter up at the farm for him. I remember him handing me that letter. I was angry at first that Bill was going to fight in the war, but when I'd calmed down I could see his point of view.

'I remember so clearly standing on the platform at the railway station. He cuddled Ethan and promised that he would be back from the barracks to see us before he sailed to fight in the war. He did come home, for three days. I was so happy but the time went too fast. I promised Bill that I would come down to Dover docks to see him off on the day he sailed. As I waved to Bill that day, watching him walk away smiling, I didn't realise that I would never see him again.'

Naomi closed her eyes. 'What must he have thought when I wasn't at the docks? Can you imagine how upset he must have been? I would not have hurt him for the world. But there was nothing I could do.'

Martha looked at Naomi. Her beautiful face was set in rigid lines and her big brown eyes were full of tears. She was silent now, staring at the cup in her hands as if it were the most fascinating object in the world.

Martha leaned over and tapped her on the shoulder making her jump. 'Naomi,' she asked quietly 'what happened to the promise to see Bill at Dover docks? Why didn't you go?'

'I *did* go!' Naomi protested. 'I got near Densole and then I was stopped by the police. They asked where I was going. They asked me if I knew it was illegal for a Gypsy to be in that area. They told me to turn my horse and wagon around and go back where I had come from.' She looked hard at Martha.

'I told the police officer that my husband was being shipped out that day to fight the war. I told him that I had promised to see Bill before he left. But they all laughed and said that they didn't give a damn who was going to fight the war. No one was allowed to see troops off and I was not going through. That was the law and I had to obey it.'

Naomi swallowed hard. Martha put a comforting hand on her arm, and Naomi went on. 'I begged. I told them I might never see my husband again. The police officer said that it was no concern of his, he told me to move along or he would arrest me and put my son in a home!'

Naomi glanced at Ethan, who was following every word his mother was saying. Naomi did not tell the worst to Martha. She wanted to keep that to herself. She remembered it though, every painful word. The people who shouted at her to get out the way, saying Gypsies always caused trouble and every one of them was the same. 'I did turn my wagon around,' she told Martha, 'I headed back to Leigh Farm. But there was nothing I could do and there was no point in staying.

✳ ✳ ✳

Naomi continued her story, remembering every scene as a vivid panorama. They had travelled for a while when Ethan suddenly tugged on his mother's arm. 'I'm hungry, Mummy,' he said, yawning and rubbing his eyes with the back of his hand.

Naomi looked at Ethan. She could see that the child was tired. 'All right, Ethan,' she said, 'I'll find us somewhere to settle for the rest of the day.'

When Naomi found a place she thought would be safe for them, she unhitched the wagon and settled the horse down. Then she made a fire and took out her big iron cooking pot and started their dinner. Ethan sat on the steps of the wagon watching his mother preparing the food. Ethan could hear birds singing in the trees that surrounded the little field that his mother had found for them. To his right was the gate. The sun was directly behind the wagon now, casting a shadow of it on the ground before him. Then suddenly a tall figure moved in the direction of the gateway, the silhouette of a man.

'Mum,' Ethan cried. 'Mum, look!' he said jumping up from where he was sitting. Naomi looked at Ethan, her eyes widening in her surprise. Then she turned in the direction Ethan was pointing and came face to face with a policeman. Naomi looked at him with hate in her large brown eyes.

'Well, well,' said the policeman, 'quite cosy, aren't we?' Then he walked over to the burning fire and Naomi's cooking pot that was now bubbling merrily. 'I've come to tell you to put out your fire,' the officer said.

'But I'm cooking dinner for my son,' Naomi replied, pointing at Ethan who was standing in the wagon doorway watching them.

'Well if you won't do it,' the policeman said, 'then I will.'

'But it's the middle of the day,' Naomi said.

'I don't care,' the policeman replied. With a twisted smile on his face, he raised his boot and kicked the cooking pot, knocking it over so all its contents spilled out on the fire.

Naomi stood there holding herself in check, not daring to do anything that would get her taken away from Ethan.

'And another thing,' he said, 'if you're not out of my sight in ten minutes I'm going to arrest you – and then what will your brat do all on his own?'

Naomi looked at the fire that was now just smouldering. 'Come on, Ethan,' she said, 'let's get ready to go.' She picked up her iron pot and put it in her kettle box, then she hitched the horse to the wagon.

'And make sure we don't see you around these parts again,' the police officer shouted at her as he strode off.

Naomi didn't even glance his way, as she and Ethan started back on the road again. The further she got away from this place the better. Then the smiling face of a man with black hair and stunning blue eyes passed through her mind, and she realised that the further she went, the further she was going away from her Bill.

✳ ✳ ✳

Martha watched Naomi. She could see the faraway look in her eyes and knew she was reliving everyone of her memories. . . memories she kept hidden behind those mysterious dark eyes. 'What did you do, Naomi? she asked.

'There was nothing I could do. There was no point in staying down that way,' she said with a shrug of her shoulders. 'So I headed back to Leigh Farm at Peasmarsh.'

'It took me two days to get there, Naomi continued. 'I stayed at The Marsh working on the farm, picking up potatoes mainly. Bill told me the last time I saw him that he would send letters for me and Mr Reeves, who always kept them until I called. Several of his pals in the army had written for him and I looked upon their writing as being signs that my Bill was well cared for. I used to collect my letters once a week because I was then working for Mr Thompson on his farm alongside the Fleur de Lis.

'Then one evening, just before I put Ethan to bed, a soldier came. I knew what he had come for. I just stood there and listened to him tell me my Bill had been killed. The soldier said that he was sorry. He gave me the telegram, saluted me and then walked away. I just stood where I was, staring after him, a thousand thoughts going through my mind all at once. What was I going to do, now that me and Ethan were all alone? But the one thing that stayed in my mind was that Bill never saw me and Ethan when he needed to, when he was standing on Dover docks, preparing to fight for our freedom in a war that wasn't really his.' Naomi stopped and sighed a sigh that came from the very depth of despair. Tears filled her eyes.

'I tucked Ethan into bed and sat there all night,' Naomi said. 'The next morning came so quietly. I didn't go to work that day, but I went and told Mr Thompson what had happened. He gave me the rest of the week off work.

I stayed and worked at Mr Thompson's farm until the end of October, but as usual the council said I had been there too long. They said that I had to move, so we packed up and went on our way again. We travelled from The Marsh to Headcorn. I knew the time was getting on and winter was coming and I wanted to get Ethan and myself to the New Forest, so we started on the road out of Headcorn. That was when I saw the planes in the sky fighting above us. One German plane buzzed across the top of us and I watched him. I don't know what it was that made me turn around and look behind, but there was another German place getting ready to attack us. I pushed Ethan off the wagon and told him to run to the bushes on the side of the road. I just managed to get off myself when the bullets came whistling through, cutting the wagon to bits. I ran into the bushes with Ethan and we hid. I heard my horse nucker and scream and I saw the bullets smashing into his body, ripping him to pieces. I wondered then if this was what happened to my Bill.'

Naomi looked at Martha, and her eyes were full of memories; and Martha thought she could almost see every one of them.

'Was that when we found you, Naomi? Martha asked her.

'Yes,' was Naomi's soft reply.

Autumn soon turned into winter, and Naomi and Ethan stayed on with Martha and Jack. Martha had pleaded with Naomi and insisted it was too cold for her and Ethan to move. Naomi had given in and stayed. When Christmas came, little Ethan couldn't believe his eyes when he saw the Christmas tree. Many times he had seen one in the window of a house as they had passed by, but he could never have one of his own.

'We always celebrated Christmas,' Naomi said to Jack and Martha. 'It was just that the wagon was too small and we couldn't have a Christmas tree.'

So Christmas came and went quite happily, and they were into the New Year when Jack told Martha that he was worried about Naomi. He said that she looked as though she was losing weight, that she seemed to be getting thinner and thinner. 'Is she eating?' Jack asked Martha.

'She eats very little,' Martha replied. 'I sometimes find her crying,' she told Jack. 'She just can't forget her Bill.'

One Sunday morning Martha woke up to the sound of little Ethan running down stairs. Then the front door slammed. Martha immediately started to get dressed. She walked over to the bedroom window and looked out. She could see Naomi sitting on the swing beneath the weeping willow tree by the pond. The pond was frozen over and there was snow on the ground. The branches of the weeping willow were bare and covered with snow. Martha saw Ethan run up to his mother. He was calling her. Then he started tugging on her arm but something was wrong. Naomi wasn't moving and she was sitting in a slumped position. Martha ran downstairs. Opening her front door, she ran out into the yard. Then she ran round to the back of the house where Ethan and Naomi were. She reached the swing. The minute she touched Naomi she knew it was too late. How long must she have been sitting out there, just wearing her nightdress…

Martha called to Jack, who came as quickly as he could. 'Take Ethan into the house,' he said to Martha. Then Jack picked up Naomi from the swing and carried her into the house. He laid her on the settee and felt her wrist for a pulse. He couldn't find one. Naomi had passed away.

'What's she got in her hand?' Martha asked Jack. Held tightly in Naomi's hand was a piece of paper. Jack read it. 'It's the telegram that told her that her husband had been killed,' he said to Martha.

'Look, Jack,' Martha said, walking over to the wall cabinet and picking up another piece of paper that was addressed to herself and Jack. It was a letter in Naomi's handwriting. 'I'll read it out loud,' Martha said to Jack.

Martha and Jack,

I can't go on any longer. I have no heart and no person can live with a broken heart.

I know all the love that I have to give my son will be given to him through you both. Jack, I know you are a good man and that you will make a fine father for Ethan. And Martha, I know you will take care of my son. You are a good friend and you were there when I needed you. Jack and Martha, you will not understand the rest of this letter for it is written in our Romany language. If you feel in your heart that you cannot bring Ethan up and keep him as your own, you must find another Romany Gypsy family that can read the rest of this letter. It will not be easy for you, because there are not many Romanies who read; only a few of them can. When you find this family they will understand. Thank you for what you did for us, and God bless you both.

Naomi

The note was in a scrawl; it went on:

Chant Muller Cannie
Pen Miri chavi tevel buonio
Kaulo ratti
Ka oatti kushto Men Dui
Miri Rye Mullerd KoRing Miri
Miro Poggard

Miduvel Del Kushto

(I just heard the song of the Bird of Death. Tell my boy to be proud that he has Dark Blood. He will have Love always. My Bill died fighting and my heart is broken. God gives you all Love)

'What are we going to do now, Jack?' Martha asked.

'I'll call the doctor,' Jack said, 'and tell the police. Then I'll make the funeral arrangements. We'll say she was a relative that came to stay because of the war; everybody thinks she's a relative anyway.'

'And I haven't told anybody any different,' added Martha.

Jack fetched the doctor, who certified the death. He wrote on the death certificate 'Hypothermia.' Martha thought he should have written 'Died of a broken heart,' but she said nothing.

'What's her name?' the doctor asked. Jack looked across the room at Martha.

'Naomi,' Martha answered. 'Mrs Naomi Emmett.' The doctor remarked that it was an unusual name. 'How did she come to get hypothermia?' he asked.

'I woke this morning,' Martha said, and found her sitting outside on the swing. She often went out and sat there when she couldn't sleep. She couldn't have realised how cold it was. I didn't hear her go out last night and when I found her this morning it was too late.'

Just then there was a knock on the door.

'I'll answer it,' Jack said.

We understand there's been a person who's died here,' said a policeman. At that moment the doctor appeared behind Jack.

'No need to worry,' he said, 'everything's been taken care of. A young lady died in her sleep.'

'Where does she come from?' asked the officer.

'London,' Jack said.

'Does she have any Identity Card?' the policeman asked.

'She has her ration cards,' Jack said. 'That's all she brought I'm afraid.'

Is she married? The policeman asked.

'Yes, but her husband was killed fighting in France,' Jack replied.

'Oh,' said the policeman. 'Everything seems in order, then.'

Jack walked out into the yard with the doctor and the policeman.

'Your old barn's getting in a bit of a state, Jack,' the officer remarked as he walked towards the barn to take a closer look. 'It will soon be falling down, by the look of it.' Jack watched the policeman, his heart pounding like a drum in his chest. On the outside he stayed perfectly calm.

'I'm going to repair it soon,' he replied, silently praying, 'Please don't look inside.'

The policeman turned back to Jack then, and smiled. I'd better be on my way now,' he said.

'Me, too,' said the doctor.

'I'll give you a lift back to the village,' the policeman said to the doctor, who accepted his offer.

Jack stood and watched them both as the car drove down the old stone road and out of the gate. When they were out of sight, he breathed a sigh of relief. It was over. They were gone. Jack walked back to the house. Opening the front door he walked through, closing it behind him.

'Is everything alright?' asked Martha.

'Yes,' Jack said, 'all we have to do now is make the funeral arrangements.'

'What are we going to do, Jack? Are we going to keep Ethan or try to find some of his people?' Martha asked.

'We'll keep him,' Jack said.

Jack went into town to arrange the funeral and Martha stayed with Ethan, trying to offer some comfort to the child.

All too soon the day came when it was time to lay Naomi to rest. There were only Jack and Martha and little Ethan. It was over quickly and they went back home. It seemed almost as if Naomi was still with them, as if her spirit was still there, although they believed that she had finally been set free. All her grieving for her Bill was over, and now they would be reunited.

❊ ❊ ❊

Several weeks had passed before Martha finally collected up all Naomi's belongings and put them in a big wooden box, leaving them in the room where Naomi had slept. As Martha went through the door she turned back to look one more time. The single bed in the middle of the room with its pretty flower patterned blankets and matching curtains had been Naomi's favourite retreat. There stood the wooden cabinets and wardrobes that she had used. Everything was the same. But, thought Martha, little Ethan was never going to see his mother again. That's when she decided that this was to be nobody's room but Naomi's. Then, when Ethan needed to be close to his mother and to find peace, he could always come to this room.

Just then Jack walked through the door, a frown hardening his weather-beaten features. 'Martha, have you noticed?' he asked, worry looming in his grey eyes.

'Noticed what, Jack?' Martha replied.

'The boy, Ethan, still hasn't spoken since the day of his mother's funeral.'

'Yes, of course, I have noticed,' Martha said, with a sigh.

'What shall we do about it?' Jack asked.

'Leave him for a while longer, Jack. He'll come round,' Martha said.

'And if he doesn't?' Jack demanded.

'Then we'll have to call the doctor out, won't we?' Martha said. 'But Jack, right now we need to make some effort. We need to take our time with him. It must be a shock for him. Remember when we found them that day, when he told me his daddy was in Heaven? He hasn't had time to get over Bill being killed. And now Naomi's died. We just have to be patient.'

Chapter 3

Just Martha

Winter was over. The weather was getting warmer and it was almost Spring. Buds were beginning to grow on trees, and daffodils would soon be in bloom. Martha was in her bedroom doing some cleaning when she heard laughter. She rushed to her bedroom window and looked out. She saw Ethan and Jack and a small black and white dog. It was Ethan's laughter Martha could hear. For so long she hadn't heard that wonderful sound and just then, his laughter really did sound wonderful. Martha could see that Ethan loved the little dog that Jack had just brought home for him. The dog was tugging on the piece of stick that Ethan held in his hand, and making him laugh. The joy on the little boy's face and the laughter in his big brown eyes was so good to see. It made Martha want to cry with joy.

'Thank you, Uncle Jack, thank you,' the little boy was trying to say, in between his fits of laughter.

'That's alright, Ethan,' Jack said, patting the boy's dark curly hair.

'Thank you, God,' Martha exclaimed to herself, breathing a sigh of relief. She stayed at the bedroom window for a while, watching Ethan and Jack play with the little dog. Martha couldn't help but smile.

She made her way downstairs and out into the yard where Ethan and Jack were still playing. 'Jack, I've got to go into town,' Martha said.

'Alright,' Jack replied.

'Do you need anything?'

'No, thanks,' Jack called back.

'I'm taking Ethan with me,' Martha said, 'only I don't know if you've noticed, but he's grown a lot lately and needs some new clothes.'

Martha saw that Ethan was properly seated in the trap and then they set off to town. The sky was a deep clear blue and the sun was bright. Martha so enjoyed having Ethan with her, hearing his excited chattering and to see the life in him once more. The child almost seemed to glow. Not a bird or any other animal in the hedgerows along the lane that they were travelling missed his glance. He noticed them all and he pointed them out to Martha, telling her what they were called.

They finally reached Headcorn, a small but very pleasant town, where Martha always went to Mrs Hubbles' shop to get her groceries. She also owned the adjoining clothes shop.

Martha parked her trap outside Mrs Hubbles' shop and they climbed down, walking hand in hand. Martha lifted the door latch, urging Ethan to go in before her. She closed the door making the little bell sound. A few seconds later Mrs Hubbles appeared.

'Oh my, what a beautiful child,' she said to Martha.

'He needs new clothes,' Martha said. 'He's grown such a lot.'

'We'll manage something,' Mrs Hubbles said. 'Follow me.'

Ethan found Mrs Hubbles to be a very nice lady, small, with kind brown eyes, which reminded him of his mother's. But her hair was black and pulled back in a braid. Ethan always remembered his mother's hair falling freely to her waist and it was the lovely colour of chestnut, not all pulled back like Mrs Hubbles'.

Martha and Mrs Hubbles measured Ethan and, while they set about finding him some nice clothes, Ethan was left free to wander about the shop. Clothes didn't interest him much, so he thought he would go and have a look in the grocery shop. Although he wasn't quite sure what 'grocery' meant, he knew it must mean some kind of food because there were tins and packets of every conceivable thing to eat, as well as bags of apples, pears, cabbages and all sorts of vegetables. Ethan wandered around looking but was careful not to touch anything. Martha got Ethan his new clothes and then bought the groceries. 'Come on, Ethan,' she said, 'time to go.'

'Goodbye, young man,' Mrs Hubbles said to Ethan.

'Bye,' he replied, giving her a cheeky smile before closing the door behind him.

Martha took Ethan back to the trap. She took his shoes and his shirt and replaced them with the new ones. Then she put his new coat on him and took him into several of the other little shops in Headcorn. She was so proud of 'her boy.' How beautiful he looked! His dark curly hair, big brown eyes and olive skin would be able to melt the hardest of hearts, Martha thought.

Martha and Ethan eventually made their way home. It was about time Jack had his tea. The day had gone so quickly that Martha just couldn't believe the time. When they reached home Ethan held the reins while Martha undid the gate. To her surprise, Ethan drove the horse and trap through the gate. Closing the gate, Martha climbed back on to the trap, leaving Ethan with the reins. He drove them down across the yard and stopped in front of the house.

Jack stood there, taking off his hat and brushing down his apron. 'Well, well, quite some young man we have here,' he said, and chuckled, watching Ethan all the while.

Martha smiled to herself. After all this time, she finally had a family!

✳ ✳ ✳

The years passed, and Martha watched the leaves on the big old oak tree turn brown and gold and fall to the ground. She watched the bare branches in winter. She saw buds grow into leaves and again and again she watched it happen all through the years. These last years had been the happiest of her life. She had seen Ethan off to school in the mornings and waited for him to come home in the afternoons. In the evenings at supper he would tell Jack and Martha all that he had done that day. He took to schooling well and was fast becoming very clever. As Ethan grew older, between his days at school, Jack would teach him the ways of the blacksmith. Now fifteen, he was becoming a fine young man, mature for his years.

Martha was standing in the kitchen cooking dinner one day when she looked out of the window to see Jack and Ethan walking across the yard towards the house. How surprised she was to notice that there was only an inch difference in their heights! She wondered if Jack had noticed Ethan was nearly as tall as he was. Ethan must be over six feet now, with a strong muscular build that still had to fill out a bit more. He had the same big brown eyes that reminded Martha so much of Naomi. His black hair now fell in curls over his forehead and just brushed his collar at the back of his neck. Martha knew that his fine face with the strong jaw could steal any girl's heart. Any day she expected him to come home with a girl on his arm, but this didn't happen.

A few more years passed and Ethan still seemed to be content just to be with the animals on the farm and to spend the rest of his time with Jack and herself. Then one day while Martha and Ethan were having dinner, she asked him if he was happy.

'Yes, Aunt Martha,' Ethan replied.

'Why don't you have any friends, Ethan? She asked. 'Don't you want any friends?'

'I never seem to fit in, Aunt Martha. I don't know what it is,' said Ethan, laying down his fork on the table to give her his full attention. 'I just don't know what it is,' he repeated. 'I feel there is something wrong somehow. I seem to be different. Their interests just aren't mine,' he said with a shake of his head. 'They talk about different things. I just don't know, Aunt Martha, but I feel there's something wrong,' he told her with all honesty. 'I'm happy with you and Uncle Jack, and I love living here. This is my home. I know nothing else. Don't worry about me, Aunt Martha, I'm alright,' he added with a smile, picking up his fork and starting to eat his dinner again.

'Aunt Martha,' Ethan said after a while, 'if I ask you a question will you try to answer me honestly?'

Martha looked at Ethan with puzzlement on her face. 'Yes, Ethan, I will,' she replied.

'The big old barn, 'Ethan said, 'what's in that big old barn?' Uncle Jack told me never to go near it. He always told me I must stay away from the barn. I have respected his word and his wishes and I have stayed away, but as I have grown older something seems to be drawing me towards it and I feel one of these days I won't be able to resist the temptation to look inside.'

Martha watched Ethan, his eyes so full of life, his face glowing. Martha could feel her heart pounding in her chest. What answer can I give him? She asked herself. If I tell him the truth, will he take the wagon and go away and leave us, and if I don't tell him the truth, how can I explain to him about the wagon?

So many thoughts were going through her head all at once that she failed to notice Ethan watching her so intently. He watched the faraway look in her eyes as she twiddled her thumbs, as she always did when she was deep in thought. Martha could see it all too clearly now – the morning she had helped Jack pull the wagon into the barn, and he had locked the door.

'Aunt Martha. . .' A voice that seemed to be very distant invaded her thoughts. 'Aunt Martha,' it called again.

'Sorry, Ethan,' Martha said, coming back to the present day. 'When Jack comes home this evening I promise you will have an answer.'

'Thanks,' said Ethan with a smile. 'I'll go and carry on cleaning the harnesses.' Finishing his dinner he put his plate and knife and fork in the kitchen sink then bent and gave Martha a peck on her cheek. 'See you later,' he said.

Martha gave him a big smile, but Ethan couldn't help noticing the smile never reached her eyes. It could not hide the worried look on her face. Ethan finished cleaning the harnesses and then decided to give the yard a tidy up. He knew it was nearly time for Uncle Jack to come home and he couldn't hide the excitement that was welling up inside him. But time passed and there was still no sign of Jack.

That's funny, thought Ethan, Uncle Jack was never late home for his tea. Then, a while later, Ethan heard someone whistling. Eagerly turning to look, Ethan expected to see Uncle Jack, but it wasn't him. Along the top of the hedge Ethan could see a policeman. He came riding on a push-bike into the yard and headed straight towards Ethan.

'Hello Constable,' Ethan said, as he laid down the rake and stood down the buckets he had been carrying. 'What brings you out this way?'

'Is your Aunt Martha home?' the officer asked, looking at the house rather anxiously.

'She's inside cooking tea for Uncle Jack,' Ethan replied. 'Is there anything wrong?'

'I'm afraid there is some bad news, Ethan,' the constable replied. 'It's your Uncle Jack. You see he was working up at the manor on those big old iron gates. He had to lift one off to repair its hinges. Then he replace it all by himself when he had finished. . . silly old fool,' the constable said. 'He should have known better! He told some of the other men working at the manor that he had pains in his chest and that he was going to sit down for a while. But he collapsed. They called the doctor but it was already too late,' the constable said, shaking his head. 'I'm sorry Ethan, but your Uncle Jack has passed away.'

Ethan stood staring at the policeman, not daring to take in what he had said. It couldn't be true, it just couldn't. The colour ran out of his face.

'Ethan,' said the policeman, laying a hand on his shoulder. 'Are you alright?'

'No!' Ethan shouted, kicking over the buckets that were standing by his feet. 'No,' he said again. But this time it was only a whisper. Tears began to sting his eyes. He dashed them away with the back of his hand. 'Why?' Ethan demanded. 'Why?' he stumbled over to his cart, leaning on it for support, trying to control the trembling and shaking that took over his body. 'Why?' he shouted.

The policeman tried to talk to Ethan. He tried to calm him down but Ethan wasn't hearing a word he was saying.

Ethan stared at the brass rim in the centre of the wheel but all the while his mind was drifting into another time. He could see an aeroplane and a horse being shot to death, the bullets ripping and tearing the horse's body apart while it screamed and cried out in pain. Then he could hear a woman's voice, screaming, 'Run, Ethan, run, hide in the bushes!' Ethan's mind was so confused, so mixed up. What were these images he was seeing in his mind? Where had they come from?

'What's happening to me?' he cried. He was holding onto the side of the cart for support. His head was bowed and tears were dripping off his face and hitting the courtyard below him. Then Ethan could hear another voice, and turning his head, he saw Martha. She walked over to him and put her arms around him. She talked quietly to him, comforting him, until he finally calmed down. When Martha let go of Ethan he slid down the side of the cart and sat on the ground, kicking up dust with the toe of his shoe while he listened to Martha and the police officer talking.

'I'm so sorry, Martha,' he could hear the policeman saying, 'but it was already too late when the doctor got there.' He heard him telling Martha all the details. She looked down at the young man who was still sitting on the ground, his face filled with pain, his eyes glistening with tears.

'Why, Aunt Martha?' Ethan asked her. 'Why Uncle Jack?'

'I don't know,' she replied, tears making her blue eyes shine.

'Will you stay here now?' the officer asked Martha.

'Yes,' she said, 'it's what Jack would have wanted. He was a good man and a good brother to me for all these years, taking me in when my husband was killed and looking after me. Oh God, I'll miss him,' she said, burying her face in her hands and crying tears that she had tried hard to hold back.

'Yes,' the policeman replied, 'Jack was a good man, and that's why he wouldn't want you to be like this. Now, come into the house and I'll make us all some tea.'

The next day dawned bright and warm just as summer days had always been, but today was different; there was no Jack to say 'Good morning' to and the house was silent, with no cheerful whistling to be heard before Jack set off to work. Ethan got out of bed and went downstairs.

He looked into Aunt Martha's room on his way down, and saw she was still asleep.

Ethan had heard her weeping well into the early hours of the morning. All that crying must have exhausted her, he thought. He made himself a cup of tea and went to sit in the living room. The first thing he saw when he walked in was the armchair where Uncle Jack always sat. it was facing the fireplace. Uncle Jack used to sit for ages just watching the flames of the fire dancing and flickering. How he would miss him! He remembered the nights they had sat and talked until the early hours of the morning, laughing and joking, Uncle Jack telling him all about the strange little things he used to do as a small boy. And then they would be up at the crack of dawn ready to go to work.

Ethan would miss him, he knew this. But it was up to him now to look after Aunt Martha, and look after her he must, because he loved her dearly; she was all he had left in the world.

Later on that morning, Ethan and Martha went into Headcorn to make the funeral arrangements. It seemed as if all the village people of Headcorn were at Jack's funeral the following week. Everybody stood around the grave paying their last respects. Ethan looked up and saw a well-dressed figure. So it seemed the Squire had come to Jack's funeral, too.

When everybody had gone, Ethan stayed for a while at the grave by himself. 'I'll always come and see you, Uncle Jack,' he said, 'I'll never forget you.'

Then reluctantly, Ethan walked away from the grave and made his way down through the churchyard. It was then that a gravestone caught his attention. He turned to take a closer look. It had a tall white marble angel sitting with a large piece lost from her left wing.

'Whose grave is that, Martha?' he asked.

'That's your mother's grave,' she replied. 'Ethan, do you know that is the first time you have ever called me Martha, and not Aunt Martha?'

'I'm sorry,' he said.

In spite of her grief, Martha wondered if she had been right not to have told Ethan more about his past over the years.

After saying their thanks to everybody who had attended the funeral, they made their way home.

On the way, Ethan noticed a group of people standing around the lake that was at the end of one of the fields at Oakwood Farm. He saw one of the men tear off his shirt and dive into the lake while another man, who was swimming in the lake, seemed to be dragging something out of the water.

Ethan pulled the cart up sharply, jumped down, and went running over to the people gathered by the lake. 'What happened?' he asked.

'The Squire's coach,' one of them replied. 'It toppled over the embankment, and it's gone into the lake. We've got nearly all the people out, but there's still one young lady trapped down there.'

'I'll go in,' Ethan said, pulling off his shirt, and kicking off his shoes and socks. He dived in, feeling the shock of the icy water in contrast to the heat of the summer sun. Quickly recovering, he swam deeper and deeper until he found the coach. But he had to go back up. He fought his way back to the top for more air and crawled out onto the bank.

'It's too far down,' he gasped. 'Give me some of those rocks over there. The small ones.'

Ethan filled his pockets and dived back into the water. The weight of the rocks took him back down faster. He searched until he found the young lady but part of her dress was tangled around the seat and he tugged on it trying to free her but to no avail. He tore again at the dress and pulled it until it finally ripped free. He threw the small rocks out of his pockets, grabbed the girl and started to fight his way back to the surface of the lake, swimming with all his might, until he finally broke through. Ethan called for somebody to help him drag the girl onto the bank, and pulling himself out of the water, went and knelt over the still figure of the girl.

'Who's going to see to her?' Ethan asked, looking around him at the crowd of people. But nobody spoke. It seemed nobody knew anything about life-saving.

'Ethan,' Martha said urgently, 'use what Uncle Jack taught you.'

Ethan looked back at the young lady, then bending down he pinched her nose and put his mouth over hers and started to breathe into her body, thinking all the while, Oh God, I've never kissed a girl before.

All of a sudden, she took a great shuddering breath and then started to cough up water. Ethan quickly rolled her onto her side and let her lie there until she seemed to make a recovery. At last, she was breathing almost normally. He turned her on her back to face him. She opened her eyes, large green eyes that looked straight at him, and were probably, he thought, the greenest eyes he would ever see.

'Thank you,' she whispered, and Ethan wondered, after the ambulance had come and taken her, if she had really said it at all. He stood up and watched the ambulance drive away until it was out of sight.

He then walked over to Martha, who was standing holding his shirt, shoes and socks. Handing them to him, she said, 'Come on Ethan, let's go home.'

✻ ✻ ✻

Two weeks passed. Ethan had missed Jack terribly and realised there was now a hole in his life that nobody would ever be able to fill.

He had been working out in the fields one sunny afternoon and came home to find a strange car parked outside the house. It wasn't just any car, it was a Rolls-Royce. He coyly slipped into the back of the house and got himself washed and changed into some decent clothes. He put on a starched white shirt and a pair of black trousers. He put on his new black boots and combed his hair. Some people thought it was too long, he knew. It still hung over his forehead in curls and brushed his collar at the back of his neck, but he had refused to have it cut any shorter ever since he was fifteen years old.

He went back downstairs, to the living room door, knocked and went in. the first person he saw was Martha, then The Squire and his wife. Ethan looked back at Martha who was grinning from ear to ear. As he looked again at the Squire, somebody else caught his attention. Standing looking out of the window was a figure with masses of auburn hair.

'So this is the young man who saved my daughter's life?' the Squire asked.

'I did my best, sir, that was all that I could do,' Ethan replied.

'They tell me it was a brave and courageous thing that you did,' the Squire said.

'Life is precious,' Ethan responded, 'hers for certain.'

'Those are fine words, young man,' said the Squire, 'and I don't think the words "thank you" are enough. Can I reward you in any way?'

'No, thank you,' Ethan replied. 'I don't want any money. '"Thank you" is enough; but may I know your daughter's name?'

'My name is Charlotte,' the girl answered, turning from the window to face Ethan.

'I would like to ask you if we may be friends?' he asked, without taking his eyes off Charlotte.

'We shall see,' the Squire replied, somewhat sternly. 'Once again, I would like to thank you for saving my daughter's life, but we must be on our way, now.'

Martha and Ethan walked with the Squire, his wife and Charlotte out into the sunny yard. After saying their goodbyes, the Squire and his family got into their car and began to drive away. Charlotte sitting in the back seat, turned around, smiled and waved at Ethan through the window. Ethan smiled and waved back, only to receive a knowing look from Martha. Ethan just smiled at Martha, shrugged his shoulders and walked back into the house. He ate his tea, and then told her that he was going to spend the rest of the evening fishing.

Chapter Four

Tucker

The next day Ethan woke up bright and early. It was nearly harvesting time, and there was so much to do. On this day, he had many horses to shoe. There was a farmer waiting with a big black stallion. Ethan went out into the yard, getting ready to shoe it. Bending over his toolbox he heard some sort of cart pull up. He didn't straighten up to see who or what it was, but carried on with his task. Then he heard a voice asking the farmer holding the stallion's head if it would be possible for his horse to be shod today.

'Certainly not today,' the farmer replied, 'they're very busy. You'll have to go into Maidstone and try to find a blacksmith there.'

It was then that Ethan stood up, after finding the tool that he had been looking for, and was taken aback to see a horse and Gypsy wagon. Sitting on the horse's back was a Gypsy man and in his hand he was holding a horseshoe. Ethan walked over to the man. 'I'm sorry I can't shoe your horse today,' he told him. 'I can do it, but it can't be today, maybe tomorrow.'

'Is there anywhere I can pull in for the night?' the Gypsy man asked.

'If you pull round the side of the smithy,' Ethan replied, 'there's a field. You can park your wagon in there, and as long as you keep your dogs tied up, you're welcome to stay until I can shoe your horse.'

'Thank you, sir,' said the Gypsy.

'Just call me Ethan,' was the reply. As he watched, the Gypsy jumped down from his horse.

'Tucker, Tucker Beaney,' he said, holding out a rough hand to Ethan.

'Ethan Bray,' he replied, accepting a firm handshake.

Tucker took his horse and wagon and settled them in the field that Ethan had directed him to. Then, a while later, he set out in search of Ethan, finding him still in the smithy.

'Sorry to bother you again,' he said while he watched Ethan working, 'but is there anything I can do to help out around here as payment for letting us stop in your field?'

'Sure,' Ethan said, showing Tucker some tools.

As the day wore on they worked side by side making horseshoes. Ethan watched Tucker hammering out some shoes and thought how at home he looked. He realised that Tucker was no stranger to the work of a blacksmith. Tucker had rolled up his shirtsleeves above his elbows revealing strong forearms, seasoned by hard work. His wavy chestnut hair was tousled and fell around a strongly chiselled face with large hazel eyes. He wasn't a very tall man and Ethan towered well above him. He had a stocky, muscular build and Ethan knew that he could never match the strength of such a man.

Towards the end of the day when they had made scores of shoes and shod many horses, Tucker stood up and looked at Ethan. A strange young man, he thought. He had worked hard all day with hardly a murmur or complaint. He was young, Tucker took a guess, maybe twenty or twenty-one. But he was way ahead of himself in years. He reminded Tucker of his own people, the Romany Gypsies. It was almost on the tip of Tucker's tongue to ask him if there were any Romanies in his family, but he pushed the thought out of his head and told himself he was being stupid. So instead, he took out his tobacco tin and cigarette papers and rolled himself a smoke.

Ethan straightened up and turned to face Tucker, putting a hand on his back and stretching. He grimaced at the pain.

Tucker began to chuckle. 'Time to finish up for the night?' he asked.

'Yes,' Ethan replied, nodding his head in agreement.

Suddenly Tucker stopped his chuckling. 'There's something I forgot to do. I won't be long,' he said over his shoulder. As he walked out into the road he pulled up a clump of grass up on his way and simply set it at the side of the road.

Ethan watched as he turned around and walked back over. 'Why did you do that?' he enquired, interestedly.

'My wife and children are in town and this is our signpost. They'll follow one clump of grass to another. If you look at the way I've laid the blades of grass you'll see the tips will point to where I am. It's a way we have of talking to each other without being heard,' he explained.

A few moments of silence passed, and Tucker looked at Ethan. Why am I telling him all of this? he thought to himself. These are our secret words and ways. This bothered the Gypsy but he spoke nothing of it; instead he asked, 'Will it be alright to light a fire in the field? We have what you call a campfire. It's the way we cook our food,' he explained.

'It's fine by me,' said Ethan.

'Thanks. Oh, and Ethan, you're quite welcome to join us if you want to,' Tucker said. 'Our plates and cups are clean and so is our home.'

They finished up for the day and then went their separate ways with Ethan telling Tucker that he would see him later. Tucker turned at the gateway that led into the field and watched Ethan open his door and walk into the house, closing the door behind him. Tucker shook his head, rolling himself another smoke. He felt as if he knew the boy. Ethan reminded him of somebody, but he couldn't figure out who. With this thought in mind, he made his way over the field to his wagon.

Ethan washed and combed his dark curly hair with a damp comb, then went down to the kitchen and made himself a cup of tea. Aunt Martha would be home soon. She had gone to Maidstone market that morning and on Saturdays she never got home till late afternoon. A knock on the door brought

Ethan out of his thoughts. He got up and walked over to the door, taking his cup of tea with him.

'Afternoon, Constable,' Ethan said when he had opened the door to reveal the policeman.

'Ethan, I see you have Gypsies parked in your field.'

'Yes, Constable, that's right,' Ethan replied.

'How long are they going to be there, Ethan? I went over to them and they told me you gave them permission to park there.'

'Yes, I did. They'll only be there for a few days until I can shoe their horse for them properly.'

'Oh,' the policeman said. 'Thing is, you know they cause a lot of trouble, these people. Wherever they go, trouble seems to follow.'

'They seem fine to me,' Ethan said, getting irritated by the constable's attitude. 'As a matter of fact, Tucker has worked with me all day, and I got a lot more work done today than I thought I would,' he said.

'Alright, I'll be on my way now,' the constable said 'but just remember, keep a close eye. . .' he said, pointing in the direction of the wagon.

Ethan watched the constable walk across the yard, stopping at the gate to look at the wagon. Then he picked up his bike, got on it, and rode away. Ethan closed the door, brushing the damp curls away that were sticking to his forehead. 'Some people. . . !' he said out loud, shaking his head and taking a gulp of tea.

＊ ＊ ＊

Martha walked towards the bus. She was feeling tired now and it didn't help to have all the things she was carrying. Still, she reminded herself, you're not as young as you used to be. Perhaps she had bought too much at the market.

Martha boarded the bus, throwing herself rather ungraciously into one of the seats, but she didn't care, she was just too tired. Maidstone wasn't far from Headcorn – ten or twelve miles – and the ride home didn't take long. About a mile away from her home, the bus slowed down.

'Get out of the way, you dirty Gypsies,' the bus driver said, rather abruptly.

Martha looked out of the window. Walking along the side of the road was a young Gypsy woman with three children. Martha turned around and looked at them through the back window as the bus got further and further away. I wonder where they are going? she asked herself. They certainly seem to be heading in our direction. Then an image came to Martha's mind, an image of a beautiful young Gypsy woman with long chestnut hair and haunting, mysterious dark eyes. How that young Gypsy woman with those children reminded her of Naomi. As the bus rounded the corner, in the distance, Martha could see the black-smith's shop. Then, something else caught her eye. Parked in their field was a Gypsy wagon. No, I must be seeing things, she thought to herself. The first thing that sprang to her mind was the wagon, the one that Naomi had left with her and Jack. And she remembered Jack saying, 'We'll keep him,' Ethan. . . She let her memories go back over the years.

Ethan heard a dog barking and ran to the kitchen window. Looking out, he saw an elderly lady standing in the yard by the smithy. It was Martha. Around her feet stood shopping bags and she just stood there staring. He ran out of the door and over to the yard.

'Aunt Martha,' he said. 'it's alright!' but the look on Martha's face said something completely different. 'Are you feeling unwell?' Ethan asked. 'You look like you've seen a ghost,' he added, putting an arm around her slim shoulders.

'I'm alright, Ethan, I'm just tired. It's going into Maidstone, and I'm not as young as I used to be,' she said with a weak smile.

'Yes, I've noticed your hair is getting a little more grey everyday.'

'Oh, you cheeky young man,' said Martha, smirking. 'But you're right, my hair is going grey.'

'I know, Aunt Martha, and it's time you started to take things easy. I think we should get somebody to help you out around the farm and in the house with cleaning and all that stuff.'

'I noticed it today, I could have done with some help. But Ethan, tell me first, what is that wagon doing over there?'

Ethan told Martha the whole story, about Tucker working with him nearly all day. Then, picking up Martha's bags, he carried them into the house. Martha followed him.

'Don't worry, Aunt Martha, they're good people,' Ethan said, placing her bags on the kitchen table. 'Tucker's waiting for his wife and family to come home. They've gone into Headcorn to do some shopping.'

'I think I passed them on the way home,' said Martha.

'Tucker has invited me for tea, tonight, and I'm sure you're included,' Ethan told her.

'Oh Ethan, I don't think I can make it. I'll have to see,' Martha replied.

Ethan smiled at her. He could see she was exhausted. 'Sit down, Aunt Martha, and I'll make you a cup of tea,' he said.

She sat down, stretching out her tired legs. Watching Ethan moving around the kitchen, her vision began to blur, and she fell into a deep sleep.

She was fast asleep and snoring rather loudly when Ethan walked over. She looked terribly uncomfortable, so he placed her cup of tea down on the table and removed her shoes. He picked Martha up and carried her upstairs to her bedroom. She really wasn't a very big woman, or was it that she had lost weight lately? Ethan laid her on the bed, pulling her blankets over her. He stood watching Martha, her face so relaxed now in sleep.

It hadn't been easy for her since Uncle Jack died. He had been a good brother to her and now Ethan knew he had to try harder to look after her. He left Martha to sleep, going back downstairs. He was unpacking the shopping when there was a knock on the door. Outside stood a small boy with dark hair and big brown eyes who, Ethan guessed, had to be Tucker's son.

With a slight stammer, the boy started to speak.

'Father told me to tell you if you still want to come to our fire for tea – you. . .' The small boy started to stammer again, shuffling from one foot to the other. Then, before Ethan could utter a word, the boy had turned round and bolted, running as fast as he could back across the yard. He climbed over the gate, jumped down the other side, and didn't stop running until he reached the wagon.

Ethan stood staring after him. Strange child, he thought, I didn't even have time to say thank you. Ethan walked back into the kitchen. He pulled open one of the cupboards, taking out a pencil and some paper, and wrote:

Aunt Martha,
I have gone to Tucker's for tea and hope that if you are feeling better later you will join us.
Love, Ethan

Placing the letter where it would catch Martha's attention, he left the house. Walking across the yard to the gateway, he could see Tucker's fire burning. He opened the gate and walked through, making his way over the field, to the wagon, Tucker and the family.

'Sit down, Ethan,' Tucker said with a smile. Ethan sat down and was handed a plate of food and a fork. He took a bite and was pleasantly surprised. The food tasted really good.

'If you want anymore, there's plenty on the table,' Tucker said to Ethan. He handed his plate to his wife and then rolled himself a smoke.

Tucker's wife, Ethan noticed, never spoke. She was not even introduced. She just went quietly about her business. Perhaps this is some sort of Gypsy way, he thought to himself.

Then, out of the blue, violin music started and Ethan was surprised to see it was Tucker's young son playing the tune. Then a daughter took out a pair of silver spoons and played them along to the violin, while another daughter tap-danced in time on a wooden board. They were very merry people and soon were having quite a party. Ethan sat next to Tucker, clapping his hands in time to the music, while they were talking and laughing.

When the music and dancing stopped Tucker turned to Ethan and asked, 'Can you sing, Ethan?'

'I don't know, I've never tried,' Ethan said, laughing.

'I bet you can,' Tucker said. 'Is there a song that you know?'

'Yes, there is one,' he replied.

'Go on then, sing it!' Tucker told him.

Ethan took a deep breath and began to sing, surprising both himself and Tucker, as well as delighting the family. The deep tones of his voice were pleasant and carried the song so well – a song, he recalled, learnt from his mother's knee.

Kamaben Gilli

Tvel gell through bory open wefs
Togor we tvel ped lods winding tober
Just yeck Gypsy dul wavero
Sar a kushto dul be tri te dul roam

So core mandy miri Gypsy bewr
Thanki miri waster be dulrady
We tvel sotty yule dur yiann ta
Me tvel kushto tut till dur end ovi yorei.

Tvel gell through bory open wefs
Togor we tvel ped lods winding tober
Just yeck Gypsy dul wavero
Sar a kushto dul be tri te dul roam.

(A Love Song

We'll travel through wide open spaces.
Together we will walk
Life's winding roads.
Just one Gypsy to another,
With a love to be free and to roam.

So come with me, my Gypsy girl,
Take my hand,
And tonight we shall sleep beneath the stars,
And I will love you till the end of time.

We'll travel through wide open spaces.
Together we will walk
Life's winding roads.
Just one Gypsy to another,
With a love to be free and to roam.)

✳ ✳ ✳

Martha made her way across the field, she now felt revived
and less tired. The sleep had done her good. She could see the
fire burning. It was getting dark and the flames from the fire
threw long moving shadows across the grass. In the distance

she could hear someone singing. It was a man's voice and it was deep and pleasant. She guessed it was the Gypsy. Nearing the fire, she slowed down. The Gypsy, his wife and family were watching Ethan, and the Gypsy man didn't appear to be singing. Martha made her way closer. When she was inside the firelight, she realised it was Ethan who was singing. The light from the fire illuminating his face made him look more handsome than ever.

Something about Tucker and his family, or just perhaps this lifestyle, had brought Ethan to life; but then Martha realised this was where Ethan really belonged. Here, by the fireside, out in the open, running alongside the breeze, here was his true home. She watched Ethan end his song, and when he had finished, Tucker and his family applauded him, and Martha joined in.

'I didn't know you could sing, Ethan,' she said to him when she was seated beside him around the campfire.

'I didn't know either, Aunt Martha,' he said, and laughed. 'Someone used to sing it to me, long ago,' he confessed, 'but I don't know what it means.'

Now Tucker understood his first impressions of the young man.

The rest of the evening passed enjoyably, with singing, tap-dancing, violin and spoon playing. Ethan tried his hand at all, but instead of tap-dancing he ended up doing a sort of Highland fling. He wasn't much better at playing the spoons either, but consoled himself by saying, 'At least I tried.' It was in the early hours of the morning that Martha and Ethan made their way home, both laughing all the way, and with Ethan repeating, 'At least I tried.'

The next day Martha was up bright and early. The song that Ethan sang was still going around in her mind. It was a lovely song but she hadn't heard it before. Perhaps he had learnt it from his mother or father, she thought.

When Ethan came downstairs for breakfast, Martha was still humming the song he had sung. She was the happiest he had seen her for a long time.

'I had a wonderful time last night,' she told him. 'We must thank Tucker and Anne and invite them here for tea one night.' Martha had a healthy glow in her cheeks and her blue eyes were sparkling. A bit of excitement had done her good and for this Ethan was more than thankful.

'If you want to,' he replied 'and only as long as it won't be too much for you.'

'I'll be just fine,' Martha said, patting Ethan on the cheek. 'Now sit down and eat your breakfast.' Ethan did as he was bidden.

✳ ✳ ✳

Tucker spent some weeks making repairs to his wagon and helping Ethan in the smithy. The two men enjoyed each other's company and worked well together.

One day, when breakfast was over, Ethan said, 'Aunt Martha, I have to go into Headcorn today. I've got to go to the ironmonger's. So, I'll see you later,' he added over his shoulder, as he walked out of the door.

He stood in the yard, harnessing up the horse, and was just about to get his big old trolley out of the shed when Tucker came walking over.

'You going out today, Ethan?' he asked.

'Yeah,' Ethan replied, 'I've got to pick up some wire fencing and nails and other stuff from Headcorn.'

'Do you mind if I ride along with you?' Tucker asked. 'Only it's been quite a while since I've been to Headcorn, and I wouldn't mind a look around.'

'Jump up on the cart,' Ethan told him. They followed the road to Heacorn talking all the way, mostly about Ethan's antics the night they had spent with Martha and the family by the camp fire. When they got to Headcorn, Tucker left Ethan to walk down to the town, saying he was going to have a smoke and look around. Ethan went into the ironmonger's. He was in there for some time getting together the bits that he needed when suddenly he heard a commotion outside and he heard somebody shout, 'Dirty Gippo!'

Ethan ran outside to see what was going on and was horrified to see two men holding Tucker, while another man repeatedly punched him in the face and body. Ethan ran into the middle of the group to help Tucker, smashing the men with left and right punches. The blind rage he felt made him oblivious of everything except inflicting as much pain and damage on these three men as he possibly could. The men retreated, leaving Ethan huffing and puffing a bit. He wasn't really out of breath. 'Are you alright, Tucker?' he asked.

'Yes, I'm fine, just a bit bruised and battered, but I'm fine. What about you?' he asked Ethan.

'Oh, don't worry about me,' Ethan replied. 'But what happened?'

'I'll tell you later,' Tucker said.

Ethan went back into the ironmonger's to get the things he had paid for and was walking out of the shop when he heard a voice saying, 'I might have known it would be you. I knew sooner or later you Gippos would start causing trouble, you always do.'

'We are Romany Gypsies, not Gippos. Gippos are your people, not mine. One day you will come to know the difference,' Tucker retorted angrily to the policeman, his hazel eyes flashing more green than brown.

Ethan walked over and threw his shopping in the back of his cart.

'Oh, Ethan,' the constable said, 'I didn't know you were here.'

Ethan looked at him with his dark brown eyes. He was more angry than the constable had ever seen him before. Then he noticed that Ethan's sleeve was ripped and hanging off his shoulder. His braces were undone on one side and his hair was more than a bit ruffled. He had never seen Ethan looking like this.

'If you had been here,' Ethan said bitingly to the constable, 'you would have seen a man who was minding his own business having abuse hurled at him and then being beaten up by three ruffians who can't see past their own stupid prejudices. And you're not really much better than them, are you?' he raged.

'I'm sorry, Ethan, I didn't know,' the constable replied. 'Anyway, why didn't you call us?'

'That's not our way,' Tucker said, as he climbed back into the cart. Ethan followed him.

'Do you want to press charges?' the constable called to Tucker.

'No, like I just told you, that's not our way.'

* * *

Ethan and Tucker made their way back to the smithy at Tattlebury. For most of the journey neither spoke. Then just as they were rounding the last bend of the road, Tucker said, 'I should have handled them on my own, you know. Some years ago, when I was younger, I would have fought them all. It wouldn't have made any difference to me. Today I could have managed one of the men, maybe two. But I just couldn't handle three.' Tucker stopped there, staring ahead of himself down the road. Then he turned to Ethan.

'You did well, Ethan,' he told him. 'You fight well, but you need some teaching about one or two things.'

'How well do you think I would stand in a bare fist fight?' Ethan asked.

'Like I said, well – but you wouldn't last any time with one of them. You're good, Ethan, but you're not good enough,'

Tucker told him, with all honesty. Ethan thought about this for a while.

'You need some polishing up,' Tucker continued. 'You need more stamina. You need to think more, and you need to be stronger and tougher. Take my word for it boy, I know; I used to fight for a living when I was younger.'

'Will you train me?' Ethan asked.

Tucker's smile was his only answer. They talked about fighting the rest of the way home.

'Do you fancy starting then, Ethan?' Tucker asked him, as they pulled up in Tattlebury yard.

'When, now?' Ethan asked, in surprise.

'Yes, now. Why not?' Tucker answered, jumping down from the cart. 'See your black stallion over there, the wild one,' Tucker went on, pointing to the horse. 'Nobody has hardly ever touched him, have they?'

'No,' Ethan replied. 'The only thing he has had on his back is the wind.'

'I want you to run and catch him, Ethan, or just to touch him. Just touch him.'

Ethan climbed over the gate and jumped down into the field. As he walked across towards the great animal, it turned and looked at him, snorting and flaring its nostrils, its eyes wide. It started to walk backwards. 'Hoh boy, steady now,' Ethan said, moving closer.

The stallion reared up on its hind legs, kicking out with its front hooves, all the while watching Ethan with wide staring eyes. Ethan jumped back, away from the beast. Then as fast as it could, the stallion turned and ran, leaving Ethan a little dazed. Ethan watched it. The sight of the animal in full gallop was awesome.

Then Ethan started to run. Taking an inside track as the stallion ran a circular path around the field gave him a chance to cut it off for a while, but the stallion was just that much faster. Ethan ran as fast as he could until he could hear his heart pounding in his ears. The sound of the horse's hooves striking the ground were making almost the same noise. Ethan used every bit of strength and speed that he had but the quicker he got, the faster the stallion went. Then Ethan slipped, skidding on the ground on his shoulder. He just lay there in the middle of the field, breathing heavily, his heart still pounding in his chest, his lungs feeling as if they were on fire.

He turned over and lay there flat on his back, staring up at the sky, watching the clouds rolling by. He could hear a skylark singing, and still he just lay there. Then he became aware of somebody laughing, and turning his head he saw Tucker sitting on the gate, rolling himself a smoke.

Leaning on one elbow, Ethan watched the stallion still galloping around the field, the sun reflecting off the animal's sweat-soaked body. The beast was as wild as the wind. How lovely it would be to be like that, Ethan thought. And he felt a feeling run through him, a feeling of freedom. He lay back down on the grass. He listened again to the skylark singing in the sky, climbing higher and higher. He could easily want to be that bird, for it had freedom too. He lay there and closed his eyes, listening to all the sounds around him. When, reluctantly, he opened his eyes again, Tucker was standing over him.

'What are you doing tomorrow, Ethan?' he asked.

'I've got two more fields to harvest. I need to get them in before the weather changes. There're other things to do, too,' was his reply, as Tucker helped him to his feet.

'I would like to help,' Tucker said. 'There's me, my wife and family. We'll all help. It's been kind of you to let us stay in your field these past weeks. You could consider this some kind of repayment.'

'Yeah, stay on. There's a lot to do and I'll pay you,' Ethan told him. 'And no arguments,' he added, as Tucker was about to open his mouth to protest against Ethan's decision. So, instead, Tucker just smiled.

'The fair's coming to Headcorn in a few months' time,' Tucker told Ethan, as they made their way back across the field.

'Yes, so I've heard,' he replied.

'My daughter, May, is coming. She'll be here the same time as the fair. I would like you to meet her,' Tucker told him.

'If she is like the rest of her family, I would be only too pleased to meet her,' Ethan replied. 'Oh, Tucker,' he added suddenly, 'the council's been on to me. They said you've been parked in the field too long. But I told them you work for me, so you're welcome to stay as long as you like.'

'Thanks, Ethan,' Tucker replied. 'But when May gets here, we'll be moving on to apple picking. Then we'll do a bit of late potato picking.'

'It's a shame I don't have any apples,' Ethan said thoughtfully. 'You could have picked them for me and then stayed the rest of the winter. Once the harvest is done, I'm left with the smithy and the few cows we have. I don't really have that much to do.' A frown creased his smooth forehead.

'Oh Ethan, I've been meaning to ask you, what are you going to do with that old wagon in your barn?' Tucker asked.

Ethan stopped walking. They had reached the gate that led out into the yard. With one hand on the gate, he turned to look at Tucker, the frown creasing his forehead still more, and there was a look of absolute puzzlement on his face. 'What wagon? I'm sorry, Tucker, but I don't know what you're talking about.'

'Ethan, there's an old wagon in the old barn, the one at the back of the house.'

'Who's been in that barn?' Ethan asked tersely, as he climbed over the gate. 'I don't want anyone going near it!'

'Ethan, it wasn't me, it was the children,' Tucker replied. The two men standing on either side of the gate now faced each other. 'The children were playing and they said they found a loose panel in the barn, so they went inside to take a look. They told me there is a wagon in there. They meant no harm.' His eyes were now full of concern as he watched the conflicting emotions running across Ethan's face.

'I just thought I'd ask,' Tucker stated. 'As you know, I could do with another wagon. When my mother died we burned the other wagon we had, and now the children have to sleep in a tent. So I need another wagon before the winter gets here.'

'But no one should go near the barn,' Ethan said again.

'I'm sorry, Ethan,' Tucker said.

'Not even I go near the barn. Keep your children away,' said Ethan, his young face filled with anger. 'You people just stay away from the barn.'

'Ethan, I'm really sorry,' Tucker said again, but it was too late. Ethan had turned and was running across the yard. He reached the house and went slamming through the front door.

'Aunt Martha!' he called, as he searched the house, but she wasn't home. He searched the farm but still she was nowhere to be found. Not finding Martha had only increased Ethan's temper, and now he was in a real rage.

Chapter Five
Charlotte

Ethan got one of the horses from the stable. Not bothering to saddle up, he climbed on the horse's back and set off as fast as it could gallop. He rode it across the fields to a clearing in the woods, the clearing to which, when upset or confused, he would always come. Here he would sit by the river and watch the water running over the rocks. He jumped down off the horse's back and sat on the bank, staring deep into the water. Suddenly, something touched him on the back, making him jump up with a startled look on his face. He was surprised to find that it was Charlotte, the Squire's daughter.

'I'm sorry, Ethan, I didn't mean to startle you,' she said. 'What's wrong? You look so upset.'

'I don't know, Charlotte. I couldn't begin to make head or tail of any of it. My head is full up with bits and pieces and I just feel so mixed up. I come here for peace and seclusion. It often helps.'

'It's alright, Ethan,' Charlotte said, putting her arms around his neck and looking at him, with her big green eyes. 'I've been meaning to thank you, Ethan, for saving my life. That day when we came to your home and my father thanked you, I didn't really get the chance. Then, when you asked if we could be friends he said he would see. Well, when we got back into our car and I turned and waved at you, he behaved like a raving lunatic. He sent me away for a while, so I haven't seen you since, to thank you. He has forbidden me to come anywhere near you.'

Ethan felt her warmth and tenderness and could smell her perfume, but he could find no words to say.

'But this is the place where I come, too, when I need to think, or just to be alone,' she continued. With this, she stood on tiptoe, and kissed Ethan on the mouth, reaching behind his head and one hand and tangling her fingers in the curly hair at the back of his neck. Charlotte let her free hand roam over the rippling muscles of Ethan's back and chest. Instead of pushing her away as he had at first intended, he wound his arms around her and pulled her warm and tender body closer.

They lay in the sweet summer grass listening to the trickling water running over the stones. A robin sat high in the trees above them and looked down. Birds sang all around them. Ethan felt as if he were seeing the place for the first time, for it was truly enchanting with Charlotte there beside him. He turned his head and looked at her. Wide green eyes looked back at him from a face that was so beautiful. It couldn't have been painted more perfectly. Dishevelled auburn hair lay in curls all around the slender figure that was lying so close to his own body. The smell of her perfume and the perfection of it all made Ethan feel that he would like to stay there forever. Time stood still. They lay and watched the sun go down.

'Pretty soon it'll be dark,' Ethan told Charlotte, 'so I'll ride home with you.'

'No, Ethan, you can't,' she replied, with panic in her voice. 'My father has forbidden me to see you.'

'Very well, then,' he said, 'I'll take you to the end of your drive.'

Leaving the sound of Charlotte's horse crushing the gravel on the drive, Ethan headed homeward. There was a bright moon, almost full. He tipped his head back, looking into the sky, watching the clouds rolling past. Occasionally, a tree with its black branches would come in between Ethan and the moon. The tree's branches that stretched out seemed almost to touch its very surface. He could hear an owl hooting in the distance. Then, in the silvery moonlight, he could see a vixen and her cubs running across the meadow. Many thoughts ran through Ethan's mind, coming one after another, never seeming to stop.

Soon, at his gate, he saw the lights shining through the windows of the house out onto the courtyard. A gentle breeze had started to stir the branches of the willow tree that stood by the side of the pond. Ethan stood still and watched the moonlight casting an eerie glow that made the whole scene look unreal. He glanced back at the house. He wondered if Martha was in bed, or if she was waiting up for him, as she nearly always did.

Then, casting one last look back at the willow tree and the pond, Ethan stopped dead. He thought he saw, but it couldn't be, a figure sitting on the old swing that still hung from the branches of the tree. He thought he saw the form of a woman. A woman with long hair that hung freely to her slender waist. She seemed to be looking in Ethan's direction, but he slowly closed his eyes and opened them again. She was gone.

He shook his head. You must be tired, he thought to himself as he unhooked the gate. Taking his horse to the stables he settled it down for the night. He walked slowly and pensively back across the yard, reaching the back door of the house. There stood Martha.

'Ethan, where have you been? It's late and I've been so worried,' she said. He just stood there looking at her. He didn't know where to begin. Martha looked closely at him; lines of worry were etched into his forehead and in his eyes was a look that she had never seen before. 'Ethan, what's the matter?' she asked him.

'Aunt Martha, why did Uncle Jack always tell me not to go near the barn, never to look inside? Today I was with Tucker and he asked me what was I going to do with the old wagon in the barn. What old wagon Aunt Martha? What is a wagon doing in our barn?' he asked her, his voice now showing signs of anger.

Martha looked at him, letting out a long and steady sigh. 'I knew the day would come, Ethan,' she said slowly. 'I just didn't know when. You asked me before to tell you, remember? And I said you would know when your Uncle Jack returned.'

'He didn't return that day though, did he?' Ethan replied.

Martha stopped there, looking at him. 'Come with me to your mother's room,' she said. She turned, leading the way through the kitchen and up the stairs. Martha stood on the landing waiting for him. Then she opened the door to Naomi's room.

'Go in, Ethan, and sit down,' she told him.

Ethan did as he was bidden and Martha followed him in, lit the lantern and turned to him. 'Ethan,' she said, 'when your mother died she left us a letter. Some of the letter was written in another language, a language your Uncle Jack and I couldn't understand. Your mother's letter told us that we wouldn't be able to understand it, and neither, I'm afraid, will you. But from that day, I started to keep a diary, a diary that turned into many diaries. Everything that you need to know, Ethan, is written in them. I think it would be best for you to read them instead of me trying to tell you now. I'll go back downstairs and leave you in peace.'

She walked out of the room, closing the door behind her. Tears ran down her cheeks. They were tears of grief, hurt and anger, now that the secret was out, the secret that she had kept hidden all those years. Martha gave a sigh of despair, for what did the future now hold? She made her way down to the kitchen, which had always been Ethan's favourite place when he was a child. He said it was cosy and warm in the winter, and when he was hungry, there was always something to eat on the stove. Martha sat there thinking back through the years to the day when she and Jack had found Naomi and Ethan. Those were the terrible war-torn days; and she thought, too, about all the happy years that they had shared together since.

She thought about the sorrow that they had faced up to and now she felt that she was going to lose Ethan.

A knock came on the door snapping Martha out of her thoughts. She got up and walked to the door. Peering through the glass she could see Tucker, standing there, his thumbs hooked in the pockets of his jacket. Martha undid the door. 'What's wrong, Tucker?' she asked 'Is there something wrong with your wife or the children?'

'No, they're all fine,' was the Gypsy's reply, 'but I think I've done something wrong. Today, Ethan and I were in the field and I asked him what he was going to do with the old wagon in the barn. He got really angry. I'd never seen him like that before, the look on his face. He just turned round and ran. I saw him come over here and a while later he went riding out on his horse. I don't know what I've done wrong, but I've done something.'

'You've done nothing wrong, Tucker,' Martha told him, with a sad shake of her head. 'What you told me explains quite a lot. Ethan's upstairs at the moment looking back into his past. I gave him some things to read. I just hope I can make him understand. When he comes down, I'll be here for him like always – and so I hope will you, Tucker.'

'I didn't think Ethan wanted us here anymore, We were going to move in the morning,' Tucker replied, with all honesty.

'No, Tucker, you mustn't do that; we need you here more now than ever,' she reassured him. 'Please sit down and I'll make you some tea.'

They sat down for some hours, talking. He told her that he had long guessed that Ethan was a Romany but thought it strange that the man himself did not seem to know. Martha didn't tell Tucker about the diaries nor about the tragic incidents that left Ethan in her care.

'Martha, what is the time?' Tucker asked her some while later.

'Almost half past three,' was her reply.

'I'll have to be going back home to Ann and the children,' he said, 'she'll be waiting for me. She won't sleep until I'm home.'

'Tucker, promise me that you won't leave until you know the full story. Promise?' she urged him.

Tucker looked at her, and the lines in the old woman's face told a story of their own. The hair that was once blonde was now grey but Martha's blue eyes still sparkled with life.

'Promise,' Tucker reassured her, as he turned to leave.

Eventually Martha fell asleep in the chair where she had sat talking to Tucker so late into the night. She was only awakened by the crowing of the old cockerel. She looked at the clock. Half past seven. She had been asleep for almost four hours. Martha got up from the chair and stretched. She glanced towards the stairs. Ethan had still not come down. She walked over to the stove and stoked up the fire, then she made Ethan some tea and took it upstairs to him. Opening the bedroom door, she found him where she had left him, still sitting on his mother's bed. Ethan looked up at Martha. She handed him his tea, not saying a word. She turned to leave the room.

'Aunt Martha,' Ethan called.

She turned back to look at Ethan, fearing the worst, almost frightened of what he had to say.

'I'll be down when I've finished reading,' was all he said.

Chapter Six
Romany Rites

Martha went round feeding and taking care of the chickens and animals that morning. A few people were waiting to have their horses shod. Martha made Ethan's excuses, saying that he wasn't well, and would they come back the next day.

It was late afternoon when Ethan finally emerged and went in search of Martha. He found her standing in the yard. 'Aunt Martha, why didn't you tell me from the beginning?' he asked her.

'It was so hard, Ethan,' she said, tears beginning to fill her eyes.

'I knew there was something different about me all those years, specially when I went to school. I just didn't fit in. I was different. I felt different,' Ethan told her.

'I'm so sorry, Ethan,' Martha said, tears now running down her cheeks. 'You must hate me, you really must.'

'No, Aunt Martha, I can understand,' Ethan reassured her. 'And don't cry, I can understand why you wanted to keep it secret so that nobody would come and take me. I know your own husband was killed in the First World War and that you've never had a family of your own. Now, please don't cry.'

Martha wiped her eyes with the bottom of her apron, then ran a hand wearily over her dishevelled hair. 'Ethan, while you were upstairs last night I had a visit from Tucker,' she said.

'Well, he came to tell me that he was moving. He said that he had done something wrong. But it's alright, Ethan, don't worry; I made him promise he wouldn't move. Well, not until he knew the full story,' Martha explained.

'Good,' Ethan said. 'I'll go and find him.' He turned and walked in the direction of the wagon, but stopped short. 'Aunt

Martha,' he called, turning around. 'I may be a while, so why don't you go and lie down and have a rest?'

'Good idea,' Martha replied, turning to walk back to the house and taking out her handkerchief.

Ethan found Tucker in the field standing outside his wagon door. Tucker watched Ethan approach. The young man seemed to be a lot more at ease with himself today and a lot more calm in temper.

'Afternoon, Tucker,' Ethan said, with a nod of his head to Anne who was standing in the wagon doorway. On the arrival of the other man, Anne left the doorway of the wagon and went to cook dinner on the outside fire, leaving the two men to go about their business.

Ethan had found this a bit annoying at first, remarking to Tucker that he thought Anne didn't like him, as she always seemed to disappear when he was around, but Tucker had reassured him, saying that this was the way Gypsy women were raised. When the men were around talking, Gypsy women would go their own way to talk or do whatever, because this was the proper way to behave. Men's talk was left to the men and women's talk to the women. Neither side butted in on the other's conversations.

'Can we talk, Tucker?' Ethan asked him.

Tucker nodded his head, taking out his 'bacca' tin and making himself a smoke. They began to walk, making towards the woods. Tucker listened while Ethan talked. Ethan told him what he had read in Martha's diaries. He told him how Martha and Jack had found him with his mother and how they had looked after both of them. He told him about his father, how he had been killed fighting in the war, and he spoke about his mother's own tragic death, a death he thought he had put behind him; this was a death of somebody he claimed not to remember, but he did remember her, the beautiful Gypsy woman with long chestnut hair and mysterious dark eyes. Martha's diaries had unlocked all these memories and now as he talked to Tucker he seemed to remember more and more. How good it felt to talk about it, and to be walking freely through the woods that were part of Tattlebury Farm.

Suddenly Tucker stopped in his tracks. 'And you say, Ethan, that the wagon is your mother's?'

'Yes,' Ethan replied.

'Ethan, you have to burn that wagon. You have to set your mother free.'

Ethan looked at Tucker. 'Do you think it's possible?' he asked. Then stopped himself. 'No, it can't be.'

'Can't be what, Ethan?' Tucker asked him.

'Do you think it's possible that I might have seen my mother?'

'I have seen your mother on many occasions. She's asking to be set free, Ethan, and you must do it,' Tucker replied, looking at Ethan with pity in his heart. He could see the conflicting emotions battling inside the young man. 'I know this is hard for you, Ethan,' he added.

'Hard?' Ethan responded. 'I feel as if I'm two people – one I know and one I don't know. The custom, the ways – I just don't know any of it.'

'But you are a Gypsy, Ethan. A Romany, just like your mother and father, and it's their way. It is the Gypsy way. You must get together all your mother's belongings and you must burn them along with the wagon. You've got to set your mother free. The Gypsy custom and ways are yours to take if you want them. It won't be hard to get used to something you were born to. I knew you were different the first time I saw you. Didn't you feel it, Ethan? Didn't you know you were different?' Tucker asked him.

Ethan stood for a moment looking at Tucker. 'I knew at school that I was different. I didn't seem to fit in. As I grew up, more and more I realised I was different'; and then when you and Anne and the children came along, I seemed to fit in with you more than anywhere else. I felt at home with you.'

'And at the same time you didn't understand why?' Tucker asked him.

'No, but now I do,' he replied.

Tucker looked up at the sky. 'We had better start walking back, Ethan,' he told him, 'only it's started to get dark already and you really should burn the wagon, and everything else, tonight. Your mother's already been here too long.'

They made their way back through the woods and across the field to Tucker's wagon.

'I'll have to go and tell Aunt Martha,' Ethan said. 'I'll collect up all my mother's belongings and then we'll burn everything over there.'

'Alright,' Tucker replied. 'I'll give you some time and then I'll be back.'

Ethan found Martha asleep on her bed. She must have been tired, he thought to himself and felt almost guilty as he raised his hand to shake her gently awake. Martha slowly opened her eyes. She had been dreaming, dreaming of a time long ago when Jack and Naomi were here, and Ethan was just a little boy. 'Aunt Martha,' she heard her name being quietly called, and opened her eyes again. Crouching by the side of the bed was Ethan, but he wasn't the little boy anymore. The little boy she dreamed of was now a man, and reality dawned.

'Aunt Martha, I've got something to tell you and I need you to understand,' Ethan began. She raised her hand to stop him.

'No, Ethan,' she said. 'I already understand. I knew once you found out who you really were that you wouldn't want to stay. That's another reason why I didn't want to tell you.' Then Martha's voice broke. She covered her face with her hands and began to sob. She cried not only for Ethan but for Jack, the brother she had loved, and for Naomi, and for her own husband who, like Naomi's husband, had been killed so young.

'Aunt Martha, Aunt Martha,' she heard her name being called again. 'Aunt Martha. I'm not going to leave you,' she heard Ethan's voice saying urgently. 'Can you hear me, Aunt Martha? I'm not going to leave you.'

Martha took her hands from her face and looked at Ethan. 'Then, what is it, Ethan?' she asked.

'It's my mother's wagon and her belongings. We have to burn them, Aunt Martha. We have to set my mother free.'

'But Ethan, I don't understand,' she said. 'Why burn everything?'

'It's an old Gypsy custom. We burn our people's belongings and homes to free their spirits.'

'But how do you know this?' Martha asked Ethan.

'Because Tucker told me. I've seen her, Aunt Martha. I've seen my mother from a distance. She was sitting on the swing by the pond where she died. She was watching me. . . and Tucker's seen her, too. So you see, Aunt Martha, I need to set her free.'

I've seen her as well,' Martha said, 'many times, but only ever from a distance. She watches you, Ethan, but she never comes near.'

Ethan looked at Martha and said, 'Go back to sleep; and rest assured, I won't leave you. I have to do what is right for me to do now, and Tucker's going to help me.' Then bending, he gently kissed Martha on the forehead. 'Now go back to sleep,' he said, as he quietly left the room.

Martha lay awake, staring into the darkness. In the next room she heard Ethan moving about, collecting his mother's belongings, getting ready to burn them. She wouldn't stop him, although she still didn't fully understand. Ethan understood and that was all that mattered. They were his people and his customs by right of birth. With this thought in her head, and the comfort of knowing Ethan wasn't going to leave her, Martha fell into a deep sleep.

Ethan collected his mother's belongings. Then, holding them in his arms, he went to leave, but stopped at the door. He had left a few things he knew Martha would like to keep, but the rest he knew had to be burned. Turning to look back once more, he left the room and walked downstairs. He met Tucker outside the kitchen door.

'Are you ready then, Ethan?' Tucker asked him, eyeing the things he held in his arms. 'Are they your mother's?' he enquired, nodding towards them.

'Yes,' Ethan replied.

They walked side by side round to the big old barn. The hinges on the barn had become rusty over the years, so the doors had to be prized open, once the lock had been removed. When the doors were open, Tucker stood staring into the barn.

'What's the matter?' Ethan asked him.

'It's a barrel wagon,' Tucker replied. 'But, good God, it's full of holes,' he said, as he walked into the barn to take a closer look.

'I told you,' Ethan said. 'When I was a small boy during the war, a German plane machine-gunned us. That's how Aunt Martha and Uncle Jack found us.'

'Yes I remember you saying,' Tucker said almost in a whisper, as if so frightened he couldn't speak too loudly.

Ethan watched Tucker walk around the wagon, running his hands along its sides. Ethan wondered what Tucker was doing, but he said nothing. There was still just enough daylight left to see by, and Ethan really wanted to get this whole thing over and done with.

Then Tucker stopped what he was doing and said abruptly, 'Come on, Ethan, let's pull the wagon out. It's time it was burned.

For a while it had seemed that the wagon didn't want to go anywhere, but after a great deal of pulling and pushing, they got it moving. With much effort, they finally managed to pull the wagon out into the field. When it was standing still, Ethan climbed up inside and laid his mother's belongings on the floor. Once more he stood outside facing the wagon. He knew what he had to do, but he just didn't seem to be able to do it. So he turned to Tucker.

'Tucker,' he asked, 'can you do this for me? I know what I have to do, but I just can't do it.'

Tucker climbed up into the wagon and stood for a minute looking around him, then he bent down and put a burning match to Naomi's clothes, which Ethan had laid on the floor. He stayed there until he knew the clothes were burning properly, then he jumped down from the wagon, away from the flames. Tucker stood beside Ethan waiting for the flames to take hold.

Suddenly, from out of the velvet blackness a streak of lightening snaked across the sky, followed by the sound of thunder. Then came small spatters of rain. The rain became harder and harder still until it seemed that the heavens themselves had opened up. The rain beat down upon the wagon. It beat down until every one of the flames had been doused.

'Come on, Ethan,' Tucker said, through the noise of the thunder and the rain, and waved him in the direction of the old barn. Both men ran across the yard and into the barn, but it was already too late. They were soaked to the skin.

'We'll have to wait until the rain stops,' Tucker told Ethan. 'Then we'll have to try to burn the wagon again.'

Ethan nodded his head in agreement. The two men stood for a while and listened to the rain beating down on the roof of the barn. Ethan turned to Tucker, about to suggest they make a run for the house, dry off and have a cup of tea, but stopped dead in his tracks.

'What's wrong?' Ethan asked him.

'I don't know,' he replied, with a stammer in his voice. 'But I think there's something here,' he said, and began to shiver.

'Why are you shivering, Tucker?' Ethan asked him. 'And what do you mean, there's something here?'

'Can't you feel it, Ethan?' Tucker asked.

'I feel strange,' Ethan told his friend, but was cut short by the rain almost stopping. Tucker looked up at the sky.

'Time to try again,' said Tucker, looking back at Ethan. They walked across the yard and out into the field where the wagon stood. Tucker walked back inside the wagon and tried to light the fire again, but the flames just went out. The wagon wouldn't burn.

'I don't understand it,' Tucker said to Ethan. 'The flames just keep on going out.'

'Let me try,' Ethan said.

'Are you sure?' Tucker asked.

Ethan walked up into the wagon and stood facing the small window at the rear, with his back to the doorway. He stood there, shivering. The evening chill and his wet clothes sticking to him made him shake almost violently. He tried to relight his mother's clothes, but the more he tried the harder it seemed to become. Suddenly, as he stood there feeling helpless, everything became warm, seemingly coming from behind him. Then something touched his back.

Ethan turned, expecting to see Tucker. He thought he might have started the wagon burning, and was preparing to jump down. Instead, he was shocked to find himself looking into a pair of dark brown eyes. Those eyes, which looked so much like his own, belonged to a beautiful woman with long chestnut hair. Ethan recognised her, with those dark eyes so big and mysterious. Ethan could understand how his father had loved her so much that he was willing to give his life for her and his son.

'Ethan,' she said, whispering his name. 'Ethan, look under the bed,' she told him.

Ethan just stood there, then he reached out to his mother, putting his arms around her. She was real.

'Ethan, I love you,' Naomi said, holding her son close to her. 'But you must set me free. Look up underneath the bed,' she told him again. 'There is a piece of loose board. Pull it down, you'll find two bags. They are filled with gold sovereigns. Take them from the wagon, then set me free.'

Ethan drew back and looked at his mother. What could he say?

'I have watched you grow, Ethan, grow into the man you are today. You're so like your father. He would be so proud of you, but you must burn the wagon. Now you know who you truly are, I can rest in peace.' Naomi looked at Ethan, tears making her eyes shine. 'Goodbye, my darling son,' she said, 'Goodbye.' Then she was gone, almost in the blink of an eye.

Ethan stood there, not daring to believe what had just happened. His mother had stayed, and had watched him, guarding him over so many years. Then, pulling his thoughts back together, Ethan knelt down on the floor. He reached up under the bed, but he couldn't see anything for the tears blurring his vision. He felt so much pain, and yet so much joy. He had felt his mother's warmth. He had felt what it was like to have his mother's love, and he would never forget that, not for the rest of his life. He found the bags his mother had told him about. He took them out of the wagon and put them on the ground before climbing back for one last moment there.

Then, walking from the wagon, Ethan lit a piece of paper, and when it was burning properly threw it inside. With Tucker beside him, he watched the wagon burn and burn. It burned as if it was covered in petrol instead of rainwater.

The two men stood and watched it blaze until the last ember faded away and finally died down. Neither man spoke. They just stood, as if surrounded by an invisible force, and for a time that seemed to Ethan to be an eternity, where the only acceptable thing was silence.

Tucker rubbed a hand wearily across his eyes and gave a big sigh. 'I'm going to bed now, Ethan,' he said, turning to look at the younger man. 'It's time I was in bed, and you look as if you could do with some rest yourself,' he told Ethan, quite truthfully.

They walked together to the gate leading out into the yard. Tucker leaned on the gate and watched Ethan walk across the yard. When Ethan reached the doorway of the house he turned and looked back. Tucker still stood on the other side of the gate and raised his hand to Ethan. He turned and walked back across the field towards his own wagon. Ethan stood and watched. The first rays of the sunrise were just beginning to appear in the sky. The first weak rays, streaking the almost velvet blackness and lighting the first places, soon shone with gold upon a deep rich blue. The first of the dawn chorus had started to sing and Ethan stood and listened. He closed his eyes and leaned back against the doorway. How peaceful it was, how peaceful it felt just to stand in the early morning light. Then, reluctantly, he left this peace, climbed the stairs and fell into his bed, exhausted.

Later, Tucker sat on the steps that led to his wagon door. He hadn't been able to sleep at all. The memory of the night before still lingered hauntingly in his mind. Tucker took a sip of tea then placed the cup down beside him and made himself a smoke. He hadn't see any signs of life coming from the house, but he thought he would take a chance and see if Ethan was up and about. So Tucker strolled in a leisurely fashion over to the house and gently knocked on the door. He was surprised when the door was opened by Martha. 'Is Ethan about? he asked.

'No, I'm sorry, he's not. Finding out about everything like he did wasn't easy for him. I've never known him sleep so late before,' she told him. 'Tucker, do you think that Ethan will be alright, now?'

'Yes,' Tucker replied reassuringly. 'Yesterday was exhausting for him, do don't worry. Let him sleep, and he'll be alright. I'll go now, and I'll finish the remains of the wagon.

You know, the iron tyres and things like that. I'll have to dig a big hole and bury them.'

'Is that what you do, then?' Martha asked him. 'You burn your people's belongings when they die?'

'Yes, Martha,' Tucker replied. 'For you see, it has to be done; it's the Romany way. Part of our religion, if you like.'

'I wish I could understand it all,' Martha said, 'and I hope one day Ethan will, too.'

Tucker's only reply was to smile and nod his head at Martha. He set about carrying out his tasks and Martha returned to her chores in the kitchen.

It was turning into a hot day and Tucker could feel the sweat running down his back as he threw the last of the earth back in the hole. He had buried the iron tyres and everything else, but the task had taken longer than he had expected.

From the steps of the wagon, Anne watched her husband. He looked tired and exhausted and in need of something to eat. So she set about cooking his dinner, sending little Johnny to tell him that she was making some tea. Presently Tucker joined Anne at the fireside, wiping the sweat from his brow. Anne handed him his cup of tea. Taking a big gulp Tucker turned and pointed in the direction of the hole.

'What do you think?' he asked her. 'Some grass seed, and nobody will ever know it's there, will they?' he sounded rather pleased with himself and the job he had done.

Anne smiled to herself. 'No,' she replied, 'with some seed, nobody will ever know.' When Tucker had come home the night before and told her about Ethan and about his mother's wagon, Anne could honestly say that she wasn't surprised. Not only did Ethan look like a Romany, he had the manners of one, too. But there was something else, something familiar about Ethan, but Anne couldn't say what it was. And. . . that song he knew!

After dinner, Tucker made his way back over to the house and knocked on the door. This time it opened by Ethan.

'Ethan,' said Tucker, 'you look like you want to go back to bed.'

'Thanks,' the young man said with a half-smile.

'I've come to see if you want me to get the combine harvester ready for tomorrow so we can start to get the harvesting done,' Tucker said.

'I'll give you a hand if you like,' Ethan offered, but Tucker just gave him a disapproving look and told him he was going back to bed.

The next day Ethan got out of bed bright and early, feeling more like himself and a lot clearer in his mind. He went down to the kitchen to make himself a cup of tea. He hadn't heard any movements from Aunt Martha's room so he decided to let her sleep; after all, she had had a few rather trying days. Ethan was filling the kettle when he looked out of the kitchen window and saw that Tucker was already up and about. The man had more energy and a lot more zest for life than anybody he had ever known.

Presently, Ethan made his way out of the house into the bright early sunshine of the morning.

'Beautiful morning. Just right for working,' Tucker said, and grinned at Ethan. Then, when he saw the young man come closer, he asked, 'Feel better after your sleep?'

'Yeah,' Ethan replied.

Chapter Seven
Rape and Assault

Tucker had already brought the combine harvester out of the shed and was preparing it for work. Ethan was glad of this, as it was one less job he had to do. When everything was ready the two men drove the harvester down to the far field and began to work.

The day began to get hotter, and Ethan's back ached more and more. He stood up to stretch and noticed almost immediately two people riding along the top of the field. One he couldn't fail to recognise by the masses of auburn hair that streamed down her back, but the other he did not know. Throughout the day Charlotte returned several times, trying to work out a time that they would all meet. Her calculations paid off eventually, and they all met up at the gateway. Ethan stopped the combine. Leaning back, he gave Charlotte a lazy grin.

'Hello, Charlotte. What are you doing out this way?' he asked her.

'Oh, we've just been out for a ride,' Charlotte told him.

'Yes, I've noticed you and your friend riding past a couple of times,' Ethan said, with a nod in the other girl's direction.

'Oh, this is Stephanie,' Charlotte told him. 'She's staying up at the manor with us for a while.'

'I see,' was Ethan's only reply, as he smiled smugly, surveying Charlotte.

'Well, I had better be on my way now,' Charlotte said, picking up her horse's reins. Then, fixing Ethan with her piercing gaze, she slowly opened her hand. Ethan saw something fall. It fluttered to the ground and lay there. Jumping down from the combine, he picked up Charlotte's handkerchief. She watched him closely. Written on the handkerchief was a message.

Meet me tonight Ethan
At our usual place.
All my love.

'Who is that?' Stephanie asked Charlotte, some time later. 'He's really quite handsome,' she said, smiling knowingly at Charlotte.

'He's just a friend,' she replied. 'His name is Ethan Bray.'

'But I saw the look in your eyes when you looked at him,' Stephanie said to Charlotte.

'Oh, very well then, he's my lover,' she said, her green eyes sparkling. She paused, then added, 'We are going to meet tonight in the woods at our special place. But you've got to promise not to tell anybody.'

Stephanie smiled at her, her sweet face giving reassurance that Charlotte's secret would be safe; but once back at the manor, the two girls went straight to the stables, and Stephanie, her cousin and friend, did not stop to unsaddle her horse.

'Charlotte, I must go to the bathroom,' she said hopping from one foot to the other.

'Alright,' Charlotte replied, with a smile. I'll unsaddle your horse for you.'

Stephanie ran through the side door into the kitchen quarters, then out into the long passageway past the dining room and made for the stairs. She didn't dare to stop, not for one second. Only when she reached the top of the stairs did she stop long enough to knock on the study door.

'Come in,' called Squire Weatherfield from the other side of the door. Stephanie opened the door and walked into the dark room. She always thought it so, even as a child. Long wine-coloured curtains hung from the windows, and a huge mahogany desk stood in the middle of the room. Bookcases filled with books adorned the walls, making the room appear smaller than it actually was. The sun never shone on this side of the manor house and the room always appeared dark.

'Good afternoon, Stephanie,' Squire Weatherfield said from the other side of the desk where he stood, his hands clasped behind his back. He turned from the window to face the young girl. 'Where have you been today, then?' he asked her.

'We've been out horse riding across the meadows and cornfields . We saw Ethan Bray. Charlotte's going to meet him in the woods tonight.'

'Oh, is she?' was the Squire's angry reply, as he turned to face the window and stare out of it again. Stephanie looked at the Squire's back. 'Where's my money?' she asked him.

'It's lying on the table,' he replied, bitterly. 'Count it, if it makes you feel better.'

Stephanie picked up her money and started to count it, her eyes sparkling with greed.

'I no longer need your services, so you may go, and send my butler in on your way out,' he commanded her.

Stephanie left the room; the Squire was still staring out of the window. Smiling smugly to herself, she told the butler the Squire wanted him. Then she went to her room to pack for her departure. She wanted to leave before nightfall.

The butler entered the study and the Squire turned to face him. 'Take this note to my footman and tell him to have the horses saddled at all times; and tell him not to let Charlotte out of his sight,' he commanded. 'This note will tell him exactly what do to.'

The butler did as he was told, explaining the plans to the footman. Then, giving him the note, with a nod of his head he was gone. For the rest of the day, unknown to Charlotte, the footman kept track of her every movement.

Later on, when everybody had retired for the evening and Charlotte thought it was safe, she slipped out of one of the side doors of the manor. She went quietly round to the stables and saddled her horse. Then, putting her hand over the horse's nose, she led him from the stables, trying to make as little noise as possible. She led the horse down the drive. Reaching the end, she climbed into the saddle and rode as fast as she could go across the marshes. The wind was tossing her hair. In the pale moonlight she looked too beautiful to be of real flesh. She rode on, innocent of the fact that her father and five of his men were following her at a safe distance.

Ethan waited for Charlotte in their special place. He had been waiting for some time, watching the water, when he heard a galloping horse. The instant the horse stopped Charlotte jumped down from the saddle and threw her arms around Ethan's neck, kissing him passionately.

'Remembering all the other times, Ethan,' Charlotte said to him. 'Think of all the times we've met here secretly, and nobody has ever guessed our secret place, our special place,' she whispered, pressing herself against him.

Ethan smiled at Charlotte. Then she saw a change in his expression.

'Listen,' Ethan whispered, raising his head. In the distance they could hear the sound of horse's hooves. 'Somebody's coming,' he said, looking at her. The horses came closer and before they knew what was happening the men were upon them.

Sitting astride the first horse was the Squire. The sight that met his eyes enraged him beyond belief. 'Take your hands off my daughter,' he bellowed. 'Get him away from my daughter,' he shouted at one of his men, 'and kill him!'

Ethan moved very fast, giving none of the men any chance to strike first. He grabbed the first man by the throat, punching him in the face. He didn't see where he went before the next man was on him. He fought him off, but one after the other the Squire's men attacked him.

Ethan could hear in the distance Charlotte's screams, begging her father not to do this to him. Then he couldn't hear her screams anymore. Like wolves in a pack, the men attacked him. All together they pushed him in the direction where the Squire was sitting on his horse. Leaning forward, the Squire raised his arm and brought the butt of his hunting crop down hard on the back of Ethan's head. Ethan fell to the ground, unconscious, the pale moonlight making him look as if he were dead. Three of the men then took their turn kicking and punching Ethan as he lay there.

'Throw him in the stream,' the Squire commanded. 'I hope he drowns,' he muttered to himself under his breath.

The three men picked Ethan up and dragged him to the side of the stream and threw him in. Charlotte screamed and tried to struggle away from the two men who held her captive.

'If she doesn't stop screaming, gag her,' the Squire thundered.

Some distance away, Tucker stood listening. He thought he heard a woman screaming and in the distance he could make out horses moving away at a fast pace. Tucker looked at his son, Johnny.

'Stay here while I go and take a look,' Tucker told Johnny. He was a small boy and he was very alert. 'Keep old Ruff here with you,' Tucker told the boy, as he commanded the dog to stay. Johnny crouched in the field, eyes wide open, alert and looking about him. Tucker walked into the wood and then out into a clearing where he could see a horse tied up. He couldn't make out what it was, but there was something strangely familiar about the horse. Tucker crouched down. Watching about, he waited. He couldn't hear or see anyone. Then something touched him on the back making him jump. Startled, he turned around. Johnny stood behind him.

'God, boy,' Tucker whispered, 'you made me jump! I told you to stay where you were.'

'I'm frightened of the dark, Dad,' Johnny admitted, truthfully.

'But you've got Ruff with you,' Tucker replied, 'and you know nobody will hurt you while he's about. Now take a lesson from the dog and be quiet.' He pointed at the dog, who sat silent at his master's heel.

'What is it, Dad?' Johnny asked.

'I said, be quiet,' Tucker said sharply to his son. Father and son stood, listening, silently. All they could hear was the running of the water. The horse stood there resting, occasionally stomping his foot or flicking his tail. Johnny looked at the horse. He thought he recognised it, but it couldn't be. . .'

'Father. . .'

'I said be quiet,' Tucker whispered again.

'But, Father, that's Ethan's horse,' said Johnny.

'Boy, I think you're right,' Tucker said.

'I knew it was Ethan's horse,' Johnny said, smiling smugly to himself.

'Stay here, Johnny, while I take a closer look,' said Tucker. But every time Tucker moved, Johnny was right beside him. 'Alright then, come with me, but stop making so much noise,' he said and together they walked slowly closer to the horse. 'He looks as if he's been here for some time. Look around on the ground boy. See if you can see anything.'

Johnny looked around on the ground, walking slowly so he didn't miss anything. Reaching the edge, he glanced in the direction of the water. Johnny made to turn round, but instead froze in horror. There was a body on top of the water. 'Dad, come quick,' said Johnny, almost screaming in terror. In an instant Tucker was by the boy's side.

'It's Ethan,' Tucker said. He dragged the body out of the water and onto the bank.

'Is he dead?' Johnny asked his father.

'No, he has a pulse and he's still breathing. Johnny, listen to me, now. You have to go to Martha. Tell her to fetch a cart and some thick blankets. Ethan's in a terrible state. Then go to your mother and tell her that we're alright and not to worry. And Johnny, don't be afraid of the dark. Take old Ruff, and remember – nothing will hurt you.'

Johnny ran and ran until he thought he could run no more. Everything he ever feared was chasing him. He could almost hear their breathing, he could almost hear their footsteps, but he managed to stay just out of reach. Johnny ran until he finally reached Tattlebury Farm. He ran straight to the house and knocked urgently on the door. In a while the door was opened by Martha.

'It's Ethan,' the young boy blurted out immediately, 'he's been in the stream. Father says to bring some blankets and a cart. He said something about Ethan being unconscious or something. I don't know, but he says to come at once. Now I must go and tell my mum not to worry. We're alright. So get the cart ready and I'll be back to show you where to go.'

'But where is he?' Martha asked, when the boy had finally stopped for breath.

'In the woods,' was the reply.

'But what was he doing in the woods?' Martha asked.

'I haven't got time and I don't know, anyway. I have to go and tell Mum,' were Johnny's last words, as Martha watched his small figure running across the yard.

As soon as Johnny returned, together with Ruff, he and Martha drove the cart to the clearing in the woods. They found Tucker sitting on the bank with Ethan's head in his lap.

'He's still unconscious,' Tucker told Martha, 'I'm afraid he's shown no sign of coming round.'

'Oh my God!' cried Martha. 'What happened?'

'We don't know, Martha. We found him like this. He's soaked through. He was lying in the stream. It was a bit of luck he was in the shallows and he was on his back.'

Tucker put Ethan on the cart and tied his horse to the back, making sure Johnny and Ruff were safely on too. Then they set off for Tattlebury.

Martha wrapped Ethan in her dry blankets, then cradled his head in her lap. 'My boy, Etham,' she cried. 'What happened to you?'

When they had Ethan back at Tattlebury and in his bed, Tucker made a closer inspection of him, while Johnny ran off to get the doctor. It appeared that Ethan had been in some sort of fight. He was beaten black and blue, but Tucker thought he hadn't suffered any broken bones or ribs. 'But we'll have to wait and see what the doctor says,' he told Martha.

'Tucker, I've made you some tea and something to eat. Go and clean up in the kitchen, and I'll sit with Ethan until the doctor arrives.'

Tucker smiled at Martha, then turned and left the room.

✳ ✳ ✳

A few miles away at Longdrive Manor, there was a blazing row going on between Charlotte and her father. Eventually, Charlotte had enraged him beyond endurance. The Squire dragged his daughter upstairs by her hair and flung her into her room.

'I told you to stay away from him. But you take no notice of me,' he thundered.

Charlotte saw more anger in her father's eyes than she had ever seen before, and his face was set like granite. Still this did not stop her, for Charlotte's temper was a match for her father's.

'What's this you hear of Ethan being a Gypsy, Father? Who told you? Your little spy, Stephanie?' she raged. 'Oh, don't look so surprised, Father, and, anyway, it's not true. You see, Stephanie wasn't as reliable a source as you thought. I can't believe it – Stephanie your spy! And anyway, why do you hate Gypsies so much?

The Squire shrugged his shoulders, turning to look out of the bedroom window and into the dark night. 'If you calm down, Charlotte, I'll tell you.' Then he looked back at his daughter, to see that she was already listening.

'It was about the time your mother and I were married,' he continued. 'The Gypsies pulled up on my land. They didn't ask my permission. They just moved in, so I went there to tell them to move. They paid no attention to me, so I went back with the police. I admit the police got out of hand and did some wrong things. So the Gypsies cursed me. Our first child was a boy. He died at birth. You see, the Gypsies told me that we would never bear an heir, your mother and me.'

'And for this, Father, you hate them?' Charlotte asked him.

'Yes,' was her father's stern reply. 'But you know, they're all the same.'

'How do you know that Ethan belongs to these people?'

'As far as I am concerned they are all Gypsies, and the people on this land as well as Ethan Bray have all got to go.'

'I *hate* you,' Charlotte spat at her father. 'And I have some news for you. I am going to have Ethan Bray's child. You see your little spy, Stephanie, didn't know everything.'

The Squire looked at Charlotte with murder in his eyes. 'I told you, they cursed me. When you came, a daughter, they'd had their revenge again. But I will show you what I will do,' he thundered, shoving her out of his path.

He strode out of her room, going straight to the stables. He threw a saddle on one of the horses then rode as fast as he could back to the spot where they had left Ethan; but the body was gone. There was nobody there. The Squire cursed, muttering to himself. Then he turned round and headed back to Longdrive Manor.

Chapter Eight

Arrest

Marching up to Charlotte's bedroom door and kicking it open, the Squire shouted at Charlotte. 'So that dirty Gypsy raped you, did he? Well, I'll have him arrested and locked up.' Marching back downstairs, he called the police. He barked his orders down the phone. 'Arrest the Gypsy at Tattlebury. He's raped my daughter. Now get him and lock him up.'

'Who is this?' the police officer asked the strange voice that was raging at the other end of the telephone.

'It's Squire Weatherfield, you idiot!' the voice stormed. 'Remember, I pay your wages. Now get on with it!'

The police used the main entrance of the farmyard. Looking across, they saw the Gypsy wagon, with a fire burning, and some chickens running about. Anne was busy around the fire, getting breakfast ready for the children. Tucker was having a shave in a bowl of water that stood on a stool by the wagon wheel, his white shirt almost seeming to glow in the early morning light.

The police officers marched up, kicking the cooking pots over. Some of the water spilled over the fire, half dousing it, and the rest went over Anne making her scream as the boiling hot water touched her hands and arms. Tucker jumped up, but was knocked back down by the two police officers.

'You dirty Gypsy bastard,' they spat at him. 'You're under arrest!'

Tucker tried to get back on his feet, but the two police officers grabbed him, one holding him while the other rained punches to his chest and face.

'This is what we do to rapists,' one of the policemen shouted to Tucker's wife, grabbing her by the back of the head, twisting her left arm behind her back and forcing her down onto the ground, face first. He then left her and marched away with the other policemen and Tucker. The police officers threw Tucker into the back of their van and took him away.

Anne pulled herself together. She must get to Martha, tell her what had happened and ask her for help. She ran across the field, through the open gate and went in search of Martha, who was at the back of the house and hadn't heard anything of what had been going on.

Anne explained to Martha as best she could what had happened; but, as she told her, she didn't really know herself why they had arrested Tucker. It was at this moment that Johnny opened the bedroom window where he had been sitting and shouted down to the two women that Ethan was waking up. They ran through the house, up the stairs and into Ethan's room.

'Ethan, how do you feel?' Martha asked, her voice full of concern.

'My head hurts,' Ethan groaned, putting a hand over his eyes, 'and I ache all over.'

'What happened?' Martha asked.

'I was waiting in the woods for Charlotte when I was set upon by some men.'

'Charlotte? You mean Squire Weatherfield's daughter?' Martha asked, her voice full of surprise and concern.

'Yes, we have been seeing each other for quite some time now,' Ethan told Martha. 'But, as I said, I was set upon by some men. I remember fighting with them, then I felt something hit me on the back of the head. I must have passed out, because I cannot remember anything else.'

Ethan looked around the room. 'Where's Tucker?' he asked.

'Something's happened, Ethan. You see the police came and arrested Tucker. Anne said that they've almost wrecked the place.'

'Why, what do they want with Tucker?' Ethan asked.

'We don't know,' Martha replied.

Later on that day, and despite Martha's protesting, Ethan insisted that they catch the bus into town rather than mess around with the cart.

They arrived at the police station around half past four. Ethan walked in, followed by Martha.

'Can I help you, sir?' asked the officer, seated behind a desk.

'Yes, you can!' said Ethan, fiercely. 'I believe you have somebody here by the name of Tucker Beaney. Can you tell me why he was arrested?'

'No, sir, I can't' the police officer replied, sternly. 'But I'm sure I can find out for you.' The policeman went on his errand, but returned a short while later.

'So you mean the Gypsy!' he told Ethan. 'Well, he got arrested for rape!'

'You must have made some mistake. Who was he supposed to have raped?' Ethan asked.

'I'm sorry, sir, but I'm not obliged to tell you that' the police officer replied.

'Well, can I see him?'

'No, not just at the moment,' replied the police officer.

With this, Ethan angrily turned on his heel and walked out. Down in the town he found a lawyer's office. After asking for an interview, Ethan told the solicitor what had happened, explaining that it must all have been some sort of mistake. When he returned to the police station with the solicitor in tow. They were able to go in to see Tucker almost at once, but Ethan wasn't prepared for the shock that met his eyes, for he hardly recognised Tucker. His white shirt was stained crimson. His eyes were black and almost closed. His mouth was so badly swollen that he could hardly talk.

'Who did this to you, Tucker?' Ethan asked.

'The police,' Tucker managed to say.

'Don't worry old friend, I'll get you out of here,' Ethan told him.

'We'll see what we can do,' the solicitor said to Ethan. After an hour's negotiating, the police finally agreed to let Tucker go. Ethan had to wait until late that night. When finally the doors were opened, Tucker was pushed violently through them, staggering on his feet, trying to look behind him to see who had beaten him. Tucker couldn't see, for his eyes were still too badly swollen.

'Tucker!' Ethan called.

'Ethan, is that you?' Tucker asked, trying to see.

'Yes, it's me.' Ethan replied.

'I think I need to see a doctor,' Tucker told him.

'Don't worry, old friend, I'll get you taken care of,' he replied reassuringly. 'What happened, Tucker?' he asked.

'I don't know. The police just went on beating me, telling me to confess. They said, "Confess that you raped her!"'

'Raped who, Tucker?' Ethan asked him.

'Charlotte,' was Tucker's reply.

'Charlotte,' Ethan echoed.

'Yes, Charlotte, the Squire's daughter.'

'*Raped* her? What's going on?' Ethan asked, taken aback. 'I don't know – but I know one thing, Tucker, I'm going to sort this out as soon as I get you home.'

The bus drew up at Tattlebury and Ethan took Tucker into the house, telling Martha to get him a doctor.

'But Ethan, where are you going?' Martha asked him when he made for the door again.

'I have something that I've got to do, Aunt Martha,' he told her.

'Now wait, Ethan, you're not well yourself,' she said.

Ethan looked at her. He could see worry in the depths of her blue eyes. 'I have to go now,' he said, turning and walking out of the door.

Ethan walked round to the stables and saddled his horse. By now it was raining and when he reached Longdrive Manor, he was soaked to the skin. He banged on the big wooden door. Presently it was opened by the maid.

'I want to see Charlotte,' Ethan said to her.

'I don't know about that,' the maid said; but Ethan pushed past her and walked into the hall. There he stood, looking around him, with water dripping from him and splashing onto the floor.

'I want to see Charlotte,' he said a second time. Behind him Ethan heard a door open, and turning he came face to face with Squire Weatherfield.

'So it's you, you Gypsy bastard,' the Squire spat at him, 'I thought I'd had you arrested.'

'Oh, you had a Gypsy arrested, but it was the wrong one. You had Tucker Beaney arrested, not Ethan Bray,' Ethan told him with hatred in his voice. Then he heard his name being called and, turning he saw Charlotte standing at the top of the stairs.

'Get back to your room!' the Squire shouted at her.

'I will not,' Charlotte said, running down the stairs and throwing herself into Ethan's arms.

'Stay away from him – I warned you,' the Squire shouted again, anger flashing in his eyes.

'I thought they'd killed you, Ethan,' Charlotte said.

'That's what they thought as well, but when your father realised he hadn't done that, he sent to have me arrested. Only he got the wrong Gypsy.'

'Ethan, I'm going to have your baby,' Charlotte told him. 'You have to know. Now we can be together, forever, can't we? Now tell him, Ethan!' Charlotte challenged, looking at her father with satisfaction written all over her beautiful face.

Ethan stood there, stunned. 'No, Charlotte,' he said. I'm sorry, but it's not as simple as that. I've already told you that there are things I want to do. . .and as for you, Squire

Weatherfield, I'll see you in court. I'm having you charged with wrongful arrest and criminal damage. You may be the Lord of the Manor and I may be a Gypsy, but you are the lowest scum.' Ethan spoke as calmly as his voice would allow.

'Get out of my house, now,' the Squire shouted at him. 'Get out before I get my gun and blow your brains out!'

'No, Father,' Charlotte begged him. 'Ethan, I know you don't mean what you just said. I know you love me really. Take me with you, please,' she begged him.

'I've already told you, I can't, Charlotte. Now I must go.' Ethan walked to the door.

'Ethan!' she called him again.

He turned to look at her, then opened the door and stepped outside. The last thing he heard was Charlotte starting to cry. He walked to his horse, but before he was in the saddle he heard Charlotte scream. Then she ran to the door and flung it open.

'Ethan, watch out, he's got a gun!' she shouted at him.

Ethan ran into the drive and almost jumped into his saddle, trying to get away. The Squire got to the top of the stairs and opened up with both barrels out of the landing window. The horse was hit first, rearing up into the air. Ethan held on with both hands. He felt something hard hit him in the back, knocking him forwards, but he managed to cling on. The horse started to gallop away. Ethan could still hear Charlotte's screams.

The ride home seemed to last forever. . . Ethan could barely manage to stay in the saddle. When finally he reached Tattlebury he fell off the horse and crawled to the doorway of the house. It was still raining hard and the rain hitting his back made him squirm with pain. He banged on the bottom of the door with his hands, and just lay there, waiting on the cold wet ground, hoping Martha had heard him. Martha walked to the door and opened it. Lying on the ground was Ethan; his shirt was shredded and there was blood oozing from the wounds in his back.

'Ethan, what happened?' Martha screamed, full of distress, 'I told you not to go. I guessed where you were going, but you wouldn't listen to me.'

'Aunt Martha, I've been shot,' Ethan told her, when she had helped him to his feet. Ethan staggered into the kitchen, knocking over some of the chairs.

'I'll call a doctor,' said Martha, beginning to cry.

'No, Aunt Martha, don't do that. Go and get Tucker, and hurry please.'

She ran out of the house across the yard and across the big field heading towards Tucker's wagon. When she reached the wagon, she banged on the door as hard as she could until finally it was opened by Tucker.

'Tucker,' she cried, agitated and painfully, 'I'm so sorry to wake you and Anne, but, Tucker, Ethan's been shot. I don't know what happened but he's asking for you.'

'Alright, Martha, I'll just get my shirt and then I'll be over.'

Martha jumped down from the footboard of the wagon and tried to run back across the field but soon she was getting out of breath and her run became a fast walk.

When Tucker entered the house, still looking bruised and battered himself, he found Ethan lying on the cold stone kitchen floor and Martha bending over him. Worry was written in every line of her face. On Tucker's arrival, Martha moved aside to let him take a closer look.

'What happened, Ethan?' Tucker asked.

Ethan's head lay on his arm, bent under his head to give it some support.

'I went up to Longdrive Manor to give Squire Weatherfield a piece of my mind,' he explained, stopping every now and then to wince with pain. 'Charlotte was there, and things got out of hand. We got into an argument, and I went to leave. As

I was outside getting my horse I heard Charlotte scream, and that's when the bastard shot me.'

'Alright, Ethan,' Tucker reassured him, 'we'll get you cleaned up.'

'My horse got shot as well,' said Ethan with a sigh.

'Don't worry about your horse, Ethan, I'll fix him up for you,' Tucker replied.

Ethan turned his head slightly, and looked at Tucker. His eyes were still swollen and black. I'm sorry about this Tucker,' Ethan said, apologising to his friend.

'Don't worry about it,' was Tucker's only reply.

Tucker took hold of Ethan's shirt by the collar and ripped it apart, pulling the two pieces away from Ethan's back. Then, standing, he looked thoughtfully at the wounds.

'You've been shot with a shotgun,' he said, 'but luckily it's not deep. So, you're not going to die, Ethan.' He looked around and then asked, 'Martha, do you have anything I can clean this with? Maybe some whisky?'

Martha went in search, and presently returned with a half-bottle of whisky.

'It will do me some good as well,' he told Martha, as he opened the bottle and knocked back a hearty measure.

When Tucker had finished cleaning out Ethan's back with tweezers and the whisky, he asked Martha for a white linen shirt. When she returned, he told Ethan to put the shirt on, explaining it would be better than bandaging his back, because then the wound could weep and stay clean. He told Ethan to go to bed while he sorted out the horse.

✳ ✳ ✳

Up at Longdrive Manor, Charlotte waited until everybody had retired for the night. Then she made her way slowly and quietly downstairs and phoned Headcorn police.

'Hello, this is the police. Can we help you?' asked the voice on the other end of the telephone.

'I'm Charlotte Weatherfield. I want you here as quickly as you can.'

'Why? What is it, my dear?' the voice asked.

'My father, Squire Weatherfield, has just shot somebody.'

'Do you know who it was?' the voice asked.

'Yes, it was Ethan Bray,' Charlotte replied.

'We'll be there as quickly s we can.'

The line went dead. Charlotte replaced the receiver quietly and went back upstairs and into the study. She watched out of the window. It was about half an hour later when she saw the car arrive. She watched the car stop and a police officer get out. Then she heard the banging on the front door. She walked over and pushed the study door open a little, just enough to hear through it.

'Can you hurry and tell Squire Weatherfield that we've had a phone call in relation to a shooting?' she heard the police officer saying to the maid.

Charlotte then heard the maid come up the stairs and could see her walk past the study. Then she saw the maid and her father walk back past the door a few minutes later.

'Can I help you, officer? I'm Squire Weatherfield, in case you didn't know,' said Charlotte's father, with a smile in the policeman's direction.

'I'm PC Wilson, just taken over in Headcorn, and you're the person I want to see.'

'Well, what can I do for you, officer? Would you like a drink? Maybe some tea before we go any further.'

'No thank you, sir,' the policeman replied, with a stern voice.

'Well, come up to my study,' said the Squire.

They made their way up to the study while Charlotte frantically looked for a hiding place. She found one under her father's desk. The two men entered the room and the police officer removed his cap. Then he looked interestedly around him.

'What's the matter, officer?' the Squire asked.

'Do you have a daughter by the name of Charlotte?'

'Yes, officer I do,' the Squire replied.

'Well, I've had a telephone call from her claiming that you shot somebody. She said the man's name is Ethan Bray.'

'Oh dear,' the Squire responded, shaking his head. 'You see my daughter, em, she's not a well person. She has a very vivid imagination. She's so highly strung. Her friend has just left and she's most upset. It was a fox I fired at out in the yard. We have hen houses. I fired, but missed him. I hope at least I frightened him, though.' He paused. 'I do apologise, officer. As I said, my daughter is not a very well person at all.'

'Alright, I'm sorry for the inconvenience, sir, but you see it was a phone call and I have to follow it up. I'll be on my way now, sir.'

The Squire took the policeman downstairs and walked him to the door.

He watched the officer run through the rain to his car. Then he returned to his study. Charlotte heard the car drive away. She went to move but knocked over the waste-paper bin that stood by the desk. All the while, her father watched the figure by his desk from the study door. He could see the top of Charlotte's auburn head. He marched over to the desk. 'What do you think you're doing, my girl?' he demanded.

'I heard everything,' Charlotte replied getting back on her feet. 'You lied, Father.'

'Yes, I lied, Charlotte; what did you think I was going to do? Now, get back to your bed.'

'No, I will not,' she said.

'yes, you will, my girl,' he stated firmly, dragging her by the arm and throwing her into her room. 'And you won't come out until I say you can!' he shouted at her, angrily slamming the door behind him.

Charlotte threw herself on her bed and cried until she fell asleep.

✳ ✳ ✳

A cockerel sat on the fence at Tattlebury Farm and crowed the morning in, waking Ethan from his fitful sleep. Dressing with difficulty, Ethan then went downstairs to the kitchen to make himself a cup of tea. He sat down at the kitchen table. What do I do now? He thought to himself. After some deliberation, he decided that Tucker would know best what to do. He set out to find his friend, hoping his choice was right.

Ethan walked outside. It was a bright morning, with glistening puddles of water lying around, a testament to the rain of the previous night. There were a few tiles on the ground that had blown off the roof in the strong gales, and branches from surrounding trees lay scattered here and there.

Bit of luck we got the harvesting done, Ethan thought to himself, as he reached the big gate that parted the field from the yard. Looks like Tucker's got smoke up, he thought as he watched the billowing mass of white curling up in the air and then disappearing into the blue sky. He saw Tucker come out of the wagon and walk over to the fire. Tucker picked up the kettle that was hanging on its stick.

'Morning, Tucker,' Ethan greeted him as he approached the fire. Tucker nodded his head in Ethan's direction. 'Sit down, boy,' he instructed.

A little while later, Ethan was handed a cup of tea. 'Only you up and about, Tucker?' he asked.

'Yes, everyone else is still asleep. How's your back this morning?'

'I was just going to ask you how your eyes are. My back's a bit sore, but I'll live. Your eyes are looking better.'

'Give everything time, and it will heal,' Tucker replied.

'What are we going to do, Tucker?' Ethan asked, with a look of despair on his face.

'Well, what do you want to do, my boy?' was Tucker's answer.

'I don't know what to do, especially about you being arrested and beaten up by the police.'

'Just leave it, Ethan. It's happened before. There's nothing we can do about it.'

'There must be something, Tucker.'

'Just leave it,' was Tucker's final word.

Ethan watched Tucker take his tobacco tin out of his pocket and make himself a smoke. Then he just sat there, inhaling deeply. Then he asked, 'Who shot you, Ethan?'

'Squire Weatherfield,' was the bitter reply.

Tucker watched Ethan playing with the fire with the stick he held in his hand, hitting the burning wood to see how many sparks he could make fly into the air.

'After that pretty maiden, were you?' Tucker asked him with a playful smile on his face and a twinkle in his eyes.

'No, as a matter of fact, I wasn't,' Ethan replied shaking his dark head. He paused frowning. 'Tucker, I have a problem. You see,' he went on, 'a long time before you arrived here I saved Charlotte's life. She was in a coach that had toppled into the lake. We were on our way home from Uncle Jack's funeral, Aunt Martha and me. Well, I saved Charlotte's life, and one night I was in the woods, the woods where you found me. Well, Charlotte also found me that night. She said she had come to thank me for saving her life. Well, one thing led to another, and now she tells me she's pregnant. That's when you got involved. You see, when she told her father he must have got into such a rage he telephoned the police and told them to arrest the Gypsy at Tattlebury. . .'

'And the police didn't know you were a Gypsy, did they? So that's why they arrested me for rape,' said Tucker, finishing the tale for his young friend. 'Now it all makes sense,' he added thoughtfully. 'Do you want some breakfast, Ethan, and another cup of tea.'

They had breakfast together and talked away the morning almost until midday. Tucker turned to Ethan and remarked, 'You know, I think the job of a blacksmith will probably die out in the future. I've taken notice, boy, in my travels. More and more motor cars are on the road – and that tractor you have there I see lots more of them around, too. I think the future, young Ethan, will be for mechanics.'

'Are you saying, one day this will all be gone, then, Tucker?'

'I think so,' Tucker replied, looking towards the road.

'Ethan, there's a *Gavver* car coming.'

Ethan looked at Tucker with a blank expression on his face.

'A police car,' Tucker said, shaking his head. 'Boy, I'll have to teach you some of your own language,' he added, with a sigh of amusement.

'What shall I say, Tucker? Do you think it's about last night?'

'Just deny everything,' Tucker told him.

The police car pulled into the yard. A policeman got out and put on his cap. He walked to the house and tapped on the door. Tucker and Ethan watched the police officer talking to Martha. She pointed towards the wagon. The officer raised his cap to her, turned, and walked straight towards the caravan. Both men stood up, watching the officer.

'Who is Mr Beaney?' the officer asked on arrival.

'I am,' Tucker replied.

'So you must be Ethan Bray?'

'Yes, I am,' said Ethan.

'Well, I'm making an investigation into the shooting at Longdrive Manor. We had a phone call last night saying that Ethan Bray had been shot. I went to see Squire Weatherfield at once and I didn't like his explanation too much, so I thought I would follow it up. What do you know about this, Mr Bray?'

'I know Squire Weatherfield and his family, but I don't know anything about being shot. As you can see, I haven't been shot,' Ethan lied.

'In that case, I'm sorry I bothered you, sir,' the officer replied, after a moment's hesitation.

Tucker and Ethan stood and watched the officer drive away.

'It was the best thing to do, Ethan,' Tucker told him when the police car had disappeared. 'Just leave it, and you'll find it will fade away.'

Chapter Nine

May Fair

Tucker and Ethan walked towards the gate. They had just got into the yard when the postman came along on his bike.

'Hello, Ethan,' he said cheerfully.

'Hello, old friend,' Ethan replied.

'I've got a letter here. It's registered, so you'll have to sign for it,' the postman told him.

'It's addressed to Uncle Jack and Aunt Martha,' Ethan told Tucker.

The two men made their way over to the house, walking in through the front door. Ethan called to Martha.

'I'm upstairs, Ethan,' she called back.

'Aunt Martha, there's a letter here and it's addressed to you and Uncle Jack.'

Martha walked downstairs and found Ethan and Tucker standing in the kitchen. 'That's strange, Ethan,' she said, 'considering Jack's been gone a few years now.'

Ethan handed the letter to Martha and told her he was going to make some tea. Martha opened the letter and unfolded the paper. Putting on her glasses, she read the letter to herself. Ethan heard her take a deep breath.

Turning from the stove, Ethan looked at Martha.

'Ethan!' she called to him.

'What is it?' he asked.

'Well, your Uncle Jack borrowed some money from the bank over twenty years ago; I remember him borrowing it,' she said, looking at Ethan with excitement in the depths of her blue eyes. 'It seems that he paid all the money back, but he never did tell me what it was for. It says here that he bought shares in a tin mine in Cornwall, and over the years profits from his shares have been paid into a bank in Cornwall. It says that the value of the shares has soared, because of something to do with tin. It seems there's a tidy sum of money in that bank! Jack had named me and you as his beneficiaries. They want Jack to write back in acknowledgement of this letter. . . Poor old Jack, he was always thinking of the future,' she said, with tears now beginning to appear. 'God bless him!'

She turned and looked at Tucker. 'Tucker, you've been sitting so quietly that we almost forgot you were there! You've been such a good friend to us these past months, that I want you to know we won't forget you. We'll buy you somewhere so you and your family can settle down.

'No, I'm sorry, Martha. We've tried to settle down before, and we just can't. It's not in our blood. Maybe we can come back from time to time and stay where we are now, but I can never settle. I shall move my wagon around the country till the day I die. You see, I don't know anything else.'

'Well then, can we give you some money?' Martha asked him.

'Yes, money would be welcome, because, as Ethan knows, I need another wagon.'

'Well, we shall buy you a new wagon and give you some money; and, for as long as you want, you can always consider the field by the smithy as your own. Whenever you like, just open the gate and pull in. You'll always be welcome.'

'Thank you, very much,' Tucker responded.

'Now, Ethan,' he said, after long discussions about the letter over a cup of tea, 'I think we need to check on your horse. Some of the pellets were quite deeply in.' The two men went round to the stable to see the horse. 'Some of the wound is a bit infected, but I think he'll be alright,' said Tucker. They walked out into the yard. They were standing talking when Johnny came running over. 'What is it, Johnny?' Tucker asked.

'We were in Headcorn and we saw some signs. The fair's coming. It arrives on Friday! Can we go, Dad?' Johnny asked, excitement radiating from his young face.

'Yes, of course, we can. Anyway, May's coming with the fair, so she'll be there, too.'

'Oh, good!' Johnny said happily. He turned and ran back to the field to play with his dog.

'He's a good boy; hopefully he'll make a fine man one day,' said Tucker.

'He's a fine young lad,' said Ethan brightly and with conviction.

'You'll be coming to the fair, Ethan won't you?'

'Yes, I certainly will.'

'After the fair we'll be moving on, and I've still got work to do. Would you mind if I went to the wood to cut some hazel? I've got to make up some bundles so that I've always got something to make pegs and flower baskets. We sell these while we're on our travels.'

'Of course you can, you know that you're welcome, and you can take whatever you need,' said Ethan with a smile.

The week passed very quickly and on Saturday morning everyone was getting ready for the fair.

'Looking forward to it?' Tucker asked Johnny.

'You bet!' the small boy replied. 'You know I like fairs, Dad.'

'Good, but you won't be able to bring that dog. You'll have to tie him up to the wagon wheel.'

✳ ✳ ✳

A few miles away at Longdrive Manor, Squire Weatherfield was also preparing to go to the fair. He had been invited to open it.

'You'll be on your very best behaviour today, my girl,' he reminded his daughter, 'won't you?'

Charlotte fixed her father with a piercing green stare, but didn't say a word. Her eyes followed him around the room.

'Leave her with me,' her mother said. 'I'll take good care of her.

'No, I want to go,' Charlotte insisted.

'Alright, I'll go and see if the car's ready,' the Squire said, leaving the room.

Charlotte's mother came quietly to her side. 'How far are you with the baby?' she whispered. 'Two months? Maybe two and a half? Well, you know there are things you can do. . . '

'I'm not getting rid of the baby! I want to keep it. It's my baby. I want to keep it! So don't ever mention that to me again.'

'Very well; don't upset yourself, we'll have to see how things go. But you will promise me to behave yourself today at the fair? It's very important to us. Your father has to open the new pavilion. I beg you, Charlotte, please behave and we'll sort things out when the day is over. You promise?'

'I promise, Mother, I'll behave,' she smiled warmly.

On reaching Headcorn Fair, Charlotte got out of the Rolls-Royce and was ready to disappear when her mother called her. 'Charlotte, remember your promise!'

The girl nodded, and walked away. She was searching, hoping to find Ethan. She walked up and down, there was no sign of him. She had just given up, when she spotted him rounding the corner by the church, driving a cart. His aunt was on board and there was another cart following, but she didn't know who the people in it were.

As they parked the carts, Tucker jumped down and went straight to Ethan. 'May is here,' he said, 'I can see her wagon from here.' But when they wandered over there was no sign of May. They were told she had gone into the village at Headcorn. The two men walked over to the shops. 'I see her!' Tucker suddenly said, with excitement.

'Well, show me!' Ethan replied.

Tucker stopped behind a young girl with almost white blonde hair that hung just over halfway down her back in curls. 'May!' he exclaimed.

The girl turned around, 'Father!' she cried, throwing her arms around him. 'It's good to see you,' she said, kissing his cheek. 'Where's mother? Where's the rest of the family?'

'Over by your wagon. We must go. But first, there is somebody I want you to meet. This is Ethan Bray.'

Ethan almost choked on his words, 'Hello, May,' because he couldn't believe his eyes. He wondered how Tucker could be so dark and May so fair. She had such beautiful blonde hair, and sky-blue eyes. He thought she was one of the most perfectly beautiful things he had ever seen. All the way back across the field, he tried to talk to her and keep close to her. She was like a bright light. She was full of laughter and joy.

'How far have you travelled?' he asked her.

She smiled at him, saying quietly, 'Many, many miles.'

When they reached the wagon, May threw her arms around her mother, Anne, while her brothers and sisters embraced her in turn. Ethan was invited to dinner, and all through it, the family did not stop talking. They were all so happy to be reunited. They made Ethan feel as if he were one of then.

'Look! The fair has started!' Johnny cried.

'I don't know about anybody else, but I always enjoy a fair better in the dark,' Ethan told them. Everybody seemed to agree. Tucker invited Ethan for a pint in the pub, and having checked with Martha, who was quite happy to stay and talk with Anne and May, they went over the road.

'Two pints of brown and mild,' Tucker called to the landlord, who came over towards them.

'I'm sorry, but I'm not serving you,' he said, looking down his nose. 'I don't serve Gypsies, and I would like you to leave the pub. I'll serve you, Ethan, because you've shod many a good horse for me.'

'Well, if you can't serve Tucker then you can't serve me. I'm a Romany, too.'

'But-' the barman began.

'Yes, you didn't know,' Ethan cut in. 'You can keep your beer, we don't need it.' And with that he turned and walked out of the pub. Tucker followed closely behind.

A while later the two men stood talking around the cart where May sat, her blonde curls blowing in the breeze. Ethan glanced her way every now and again. She was so distracting, he thought.

Suddenly, from the corner of his eye, Ethan saw a woman with a parasol. She had bright auburn hair. He thought she looked familiar; it couldn't be. . . Oh my God, Charlotte! He thought. I must be seeing things. May spoke to Ethan and he took a step closer to her. Charlotte became enraged, and even more so when May reached down and brushed a curl away from Ethan's eyes. Charlotte was so angry that she walked quickly alongside the horse and smacked it as hard she could with her parasol. The horse reared up and then bolted, taking May and the cart with it.

Ethan jumped out of the way, but, scrambling to his feet, grabbed the back of the cart just in time. He was being dragged along, but he pulled himself up into the cart. May was trying to hold the reins, with difficulty. She screamed for help. Ethan tried to find his balance as he made his way down the cart. He jumped onto the seat. 'Give me the reins!' May tried to, but one of them dropped, and was dragging on the ground by the wheel. The other was resting on the shafts. Ethan jumped onto the front board of the cart, shouting, 'Hold on, May!'

He watched the horse's mane blowing in the wind, almost mesmerising him. As he jumped further forward onto the shafts, he slipped. He could not quite reach, and he ended up hanging half on and half off the shafts. He looked down and saw the horses hooves barely missing his feet as they stomped along the ground. Slowly, Ethan managed to drag himself up, and hauled himself onto the back of the horse. He leaned forward, trying to pull the horse back by grabbing either side of the bridle. At the same moment, the dragging rein got caught in the axle and the wheel skidded. The cart tipped over, throwing May clear, but falling on Ethan. She had landed on the grass verge. Ethan saw everyone running towards them. Martha was screaming for help. Tucker and some of the other men arrived first, and lifted the cart off Ethan. He was still conscious, and the raw skin of his hand was stinging painfully.

'Are *you* alright?' asked May, crouching down beside him.

'Are *you* alright, May? I thought the cart had turned over on top of you. I couldn't see you when I turned back!' His brown eyes were wide in pain and confusion.

'Your hand is bleeding, Ethan. Look away – I'll use some of my petticoat.'

Lifting her long blue dress, she tore a strip from her white petticoat, and bound the cloth around his fingers. As she wiped the blood from the centre of his palm, her movements suddenly slowed down. 'You are one of us,' she whispered in surprise. 'You have the dark blood.'

Ethan said nothing. He was staring intently into May's sky-blue eyes. He was spellbound. His eyes could not leave hers.

May stood up and brushed herself down. 'Can you walk?' she asked.

Tucker and another man helped Ethan to his feet, but he was limping. Martha was just about to fuss around him when Ethan said, 'It's nothing to worry about, I'll manage. My leg hurts a bit, but it's probably from where I've been sitting on the shaft.'

People were rushing about trying to right the cart. Ethan limped over to the horse. It was dead. One of the shafts had snapped and stabbed the horse in its side. Ethan shook his head, hoping the beautiful animal had been killed instantly. It was such a terrible thing to have happened.

'I'm so sorry about your horse, May. You can have one of mine from the farm,' he told her.

'Don't worry,' May said, as they strolled back around the church, side by side.

'I wonder what made the horse bolt, he had never done that before. Something must really have spooked him.'

As they walked on toward the field, Ethan suddenly had the feeling that someone was watching them. He looked across the field to where the carts were parked. A young man of about his own age was leaning against the back of a flat cart. May moved across to him.

'Ethan,' she said, 'Here is someone I want you to meet. This is Cornelius Lee.'

Ethan held out his hand in a gesture of friendship, but Cornelius looked away.

'Until now,' May continued, her eyes glaring in warning, 'Cornelius has been a good friend of mine.'

She then helped Ethan into the back of his cart to rest for a while. Martha came over, fussing, insisting that Ethan see the doctor she had summoned.

'I'm alright,' Ethan protested, but Martha was having none of it.'

'Can I talk to you, May?' Cornelius asked.

'I will wait until the doctor has been,' said May, not leaving Ethan's side. 'Is it important?'

'Well, it can wait, I suppose,' he replied, and strolled away in a huff.

'Are you badly hurt?' she asked Ethan.

'I'm alright, it's nothing serious,' he insisted; but May did not want to leave until the doctor had checked him over. Then he said, 'You had better go, May, your man friend is waiting for you still.'

'Friend!' said May. 'I *thought* that's what he was!'

Soon the doctor arrived, and while being attended to, Ethan watched as May and Cornelius threaded their way into the crowd. He could see they were arguing. May was throwing her arms about, and Cornelius was pointing as they headed towards the wagons. Ethan would have loved to have heard what they were saying, but they were too far away.

'Hold still!' said Dr Hardcastle, 'I'm trying to bandage your hand. You will have to rest it for a bit. I would say that you have torn a few ligaments. No strenuous work, mind!'

'How much do we owe you?' Tucker asked. The doctor looked bemused, 'Who is this?'

'This,' said Ethan with a smile, 'This is Tucker Beaney.'

'What do you mean payment, Mr Beaney? Ethan's my patient; he does not have to pay.'

'We always have to pay a doctor when we call one out.'

'Well, you don't have to pay me!' said the doctor with a puzzled expression.

✳ ✳ ✳

Over by the wagons, May and Cornelius were in a full-scale argument.

'So this is what you do behind my back, is it, May Beaney?' Cornelius protested.

'What do you mean, "behind your back"?' hissed May, with a wild look in her eye. 'I do nothing that gives you the right to order me around!'

'You're my woman!' shouted Cornelius.

'I'm yours, am I?' May retorted, standing with her hands on her hips, her hair blowing across her angry face. 'I belong to no one. I do as I please, exactly as I like!'

'But,' began Cornelius, 'I have always taken it that we are betrothed. We've known each other all our lives.' His face filled with a mean look of possession.

'Well,' May answered, incensed, 'you can unbetroth yourself. I would not think about being betrothed to you if you were the last person on this earth!'

'So, it's Ethan Bray now, is it?'

'Don't you even speak his name. You would never be able to walk in his shoes. He is a better man than you, any day!'

Cornelius was whipped into a fury. He punched the back of the wagon, splitting one of the boards in two.

'When his hand is better, we will see. I'll wait until his hand is better, so when I beat him to the ground you will not be able to say that I took advantage,' said Cornelius, looking viciously at May. She reached her hand out to slap him, but he grabbed her arms and pulled her towards him, in a bear-hug. He pressed his mouth violently on hers, kissing her, even as she twisted her head from side to side. She struggled and stuck her fingers into his ribs, and pushed with all her strength. Cornelius let go with a cry of pain.

'Get away from me, you swine!' May shouted.

'There is only one way he can have you, May, and that is if he wins – and believe me, there will be no Ethan Bray winning your hand,' boasted Cornelius.

Suddenly he lunged at her, and grabbing her, pushed her under the wagon.

'I'll be the only man that you're gonna have, May,' he hissed, as he began to tear at her clothes.

At that moment he was grabbed from behind, and dragged from under the wagon. It was Cornelius's grandfather, Joe.

'What kind of behaviour is this?' he bellowed. 'Down on all fours! You behave like an animal, you'll be treated like an animal.' He slashed at Cornelius with a horsewhip. 'Now, crawl. Crawl to your horse and get out of my sight!' Joe shouted fiercely.

Joe watched Cornelius ride away, and he turned to May. She was sitting by the wagon, pulling her torn clothes around her bared body. Joe reached inside for a blanket and covered May with it. He made her some tea and sat beside her. 'Whatever happened?' he asked.

'He went like a wild animal. He's jealous you see, jealous of Ethan Bray.'

'Who is that?'

'It's a long story, Uncle.' She used the term politely. 'Well take your time,' he said, sipping his tea. 'I'll listen.'

Later that day, after May had thanked Joe for his help, and changed her dress, she left the fairground to find Tattlebury Farm. As she set off a voice called out behind her. It was Johnny, her brother. He told her that Ethan had gone with their mother and father, and he showed her the way to go. On arrival, she found Tucker and Anne, together with Martha and Ethan, sitting around a fire, talking. As soon as Anne saw her daughter, she jumped to her feet, asking, 'May, whatever happened?'

May sat down and explained. Tucker became very angry.

'Uncle Joe has sorted it. He gave Cornelius a whipping and sent him on his way.'

'That's not enough,' said Tucker, strutting up and down. 'I'll have to fight him.'

'No,' said Ethan quietly, 'I'll fight him.' He stood up. 'After all, this was because of me, am I right, May?' She nodded.

'I'll fight him for your honour, May, and for you!' He read the words behind her eyes.

'He's never been beaten in a fight, Ethan,' Tucker interrupted. 'I'll arrange the fight, but it will have to be at least six weeks from now. Give your hand a chance to heal up. Don't worry about the farm chores, we'll see to that. You just fix on getting your hand well.'

Chapter Ten

The Fight

Over the next few weeks Ethan's hand began to heal, and every day he practised sparring with Tucker. They would run together, and this improved Ethan's fitness.

Soon Tucker said, with a big smile on his face, 'Not much more to do, and you'll be ready. I'm really looking forward to this fight.'

'Nothing like a good fight to gladden the soul, eh?' remarked Ethan.

All during these weeks, Ethan and May had been seeing each other, and found themselves drawn more and more towards each other, and May had pulled her wagon into the field next to her father's, to be close. He had repaired the wagon, and Ethan had provided a good horse. Ethan found her fascinating, and watched her as often as he could. Sometimes Tucker spotted him, and would laugh and shake his head.

Finally Tucker said, 'You're ready, Ethan. I shall go and see Joe tomorrow to get everything arranged. What size shoe do you take? I want to buy you a new pair with a good tread.'

'Size eleven,' replied Ethan.

'Good. I think you should fight on the grass, not on the road; that way, if you go down, you won't do so much damage.'

Tucker arranged the fight for the next week, in the field at Tattlebury. All was set.

During the following days, Ethan spent as much time with May as he could. He told her everything about himself and all about his life that he could remember. The one thing he left out was about Charlotte. He decided that this would be best left for another time. The night before the fight came, there was a lot of tension and nervousness at Tattlebury. Ethan and

May sat at the fire with the stars for company. They talked for a while, and then May became silent.

'What is it, May?' asked Ethan.

She looked at him with her steady gaze: 'I love you, Ethan Bray.' She hardly believed that she had said it.

'I know that I love you, too, May, but I didn't like to say. I've felt too awkward.' Ethan reached to put his arm around her, and pulled her closer to his side.

'Do you sing, Ethan?' she asked.

'Well, maybe a little.'

'Then sing with me,' she said.

They began an old love song which, somehow, Ethan recognised. Their voices were not quite in tune, but they did not care, for their hearts, it seemed, were in perfect harmony.

✳ ✳ ✳

The morning of the fight arrived. They were surprised to see that a large crowd of people had turned up. It seemed as if most of Headcorn were there, and all the Romany people from the fair. Last to arrive was Cornelius, and his grandfather, Joe. The fight was to begin.

'Well, if it ain't the big man himself!' scoffed Cornelius, grinning, and turning to face Ethan.

'It's a fight you want, Cornelius. So look no further,' Ethan said clearly and stepped forward.

'What's it going to be? Clean or - ?'

With that, crack! Came a left fist slammed into Ethan's face, followed by a right. Ethan stumbled back, but kept on his feet. Then he rushed forward head-long, and punched Cornelius straight in the stomach, following with a sharp uppercut to the chin. Both men backed off, circling. Cornelius swung a left, catching Ethan on the side of his head, knocking him sideways. He followed this with another sharp left to

Ethan's face, but Ethan ducked and managed to punch Cornelius in the mouth, cutting his lip.

Cornelius was taken by surprise. He was raging and rushed forward, but Ethan was faster, ducking and diving, throwing lefts and rights. Cornelius drew breath, and recovering his wits, he caught Ethan with a heavy blow. Ethan went down on his back, blood began streaming down his face from a cut eye. This filled him with a new fervour. He was back on his feet and fighting furiously. Cornelius stumbled back, wiping blood from his face, staring at Ethan with hell raging in his eyes.

'Now I'm going to kill you,' he screamed, exploding with anger.

The two men faced each other, toe to toe, enticing and punching, until Cornelius, grabbing Ethan by the waist, lifted him from the ground, crushing him in a bear-hug. Pain shot through Ethan's back, but he managed to head-butt Cornelius on the nose. The grip loosened, and Ethan broke free. As Cornelius reeled, Ethan was at him shouting 'Have you had enough yet?'

'Like hell I have!' spluttered Cornelius. The two men circled each other like tired animals, bloody now and looking for a way to finish. Ethan suddenly threw a wild left, catching Cornelius in the stomach, knocking the wind out of him. Cornelius went down, hitting the ground. He rolled over and lay spread-eagled. Joe and another man picked him up and carried him to the side. They threw water over him. On the other side of the circle, a clean white piece of linen was held to Ethan's eye, to try and stop the bleeding.

Tucker called for a shake of hands, but Cornelius refused, pushing the surprised Tucker to the ground. Ethan was on his feet, trying to defend himself, but Tucker stepped between the two men and stopped the fight. Blood was still streaming down Ethan's face, and Cornelius looked as if he was on the verge of collapsing. Even so, he pushed Tucker away, and fighting his way through the crowd, knocked people all over the place in his rage. He made his way to his cart, and rode out of Tattlebury like a man possessed by some inner demon.

'Let me take a look at that eye,' Tucker said to Ethan. 'Now don't worry anymore about him. Hmm, I'm afraid you are going to need stitches. I could do it for you, or we could take you down to the local doctor.'

Ethan told Tucker he wanted him to do it, and Tucker gathered the necessary bits and pieces. He stitched the skin carefully.

'That should do,' he said cutting the last thread. 'it should heal without too much of a scar. It's in your eyebrow really, so no one will see it.'

By now the crowd had begun to dwindle away, still talking about the fight, framing up and throwing dummy punches.

'It'll be a fight; that's remembered for many a year,' declared Tucker, grinning proudly. 'It was one of the best. . . a real battle.'

'Cornelius should never have done what he did!' exclaimed Ethan.

'You're right,' said Tucker, 'but you have to understand. Cornelius didn't just lose the fight he lost somebody that he has loved all his life. See, even I thought that May would end up marrying him. Well, that's how things go.'

For a moment Ethan looked troubled.

'What is it?' asked Tucker, seeing the boy's look.

'I haven't asked May yet, but I think I'd better ask you first. Can I have the hand of May in marriage?'

'With all my blessings,' pronounced Tucker, with a laugh. 'You two would be ideally suited. Besides, it would be nice to see her calm down a little, not lead quite such a spirited life. I worry about her, not knowing where she is half the time.'

They began strolling back to the wagons. Ethan was thanking Tucker for the fine shoes he gave him for the fight, when he heard his name being called. It was May, she was running towards him.

'I knew you would win,' she said breathlessly, her hair hanging loose and wild down her back. At that moment Ethan thought that he had never seen her look more beautiful.

She lifted her arms and flung them around his neck. 'I just knew you would win,' she said again, holding him close.

'I have just asked your father, and now May, I'm asking you. Will you marry me?'

May looked shyly to her father and then back to Ethan. 'Of course I will,' she whispered, her cheeks glowing red. They all laughed as they made their way over to the wagons for tea. May was walking on air between the two men she loved most in all the world.

After tea, Tucker watched the happy couple leave to go over to the house to tell Martha the good news. I sure hope Ethan can tame her a little, for she is a wild one, he thought.

When they arrived at the house Martha was not there, so they sat and waited. Ethan leaned across the kitchen table, saying, 'May, there's something I have to tell you.'

May took his hand, and replied, 'I'm so happy, you know, I've never been this happy.'

'May, I have to tell you,' Ethan continued. 'Please listen to me. I can't put it off any longer; it wouldn't be fair.'

May listened without saying a word, as Ethan told her all about Charlotte, and their unborn baby, how they met and all that had happened. May's face remained calm and still, but tears began to roll down her cheeks. Then she rose slowly from the table and walked to the door. Flinging it wide open, she began to run.

'May!' Ethan called after her, but she didn't seem to hear him. He watched her run down to the gate and across the field to her wagon. Ethan decided it was best to leave her for a bit, till tomorrow morning. Then, he thought, he could get up and sort out the mess.

Just then Martha came home. 'Penny for them,' she called cheerily.

'Oh, it's nothing,' replied Ethan. 'I'm just tired. I'm going to lie down.'

Chapter Eleven
Travelling Home

As usual, it was the cockerel crowing the next morning that woke Ethan. He dressed quickly and went downstairs, little knowing how many times that night Martha had checked him, still worrying about the blows he had had from the fight. But Ethan was strong. He said that he would skip breakfast and was out of the door in a flash.

'Poor Ethan,' said Martha, shaking her head.

As soon as he looked across from the yard he saw that a wagon was missing – May's wagon. He started to run across the field, 'Where is she?' he called to Tucker.

'You should have told her from the beginning,' Tucker said slowly.

'I tried,' stammered Ethan, 'but I just couldn't do it. I wish to God Charlotte and me had never happened.'

'But it did. Don't worry, she hasn't gone alone, Johnny has gone with her.'

'Where has she gone?'

'I don't know. She said she needed time to sort things out in her head and travelling helps her to do that.'

'I didn't hear the wagon go across the yard,' Ethan said to Tucker.

'She went across the field and out through the top gate so she wouldn't wake you.'

Ethan did not reply. He just stood there in silence.

'How can I find her, Tucker?' he asked after a while.

'Just let May think this one over, Ethan, and she'll come back when she's good and ready.'

'And what if she doesn't come back?'

'That will be her decision,' Tucker told him.

Day after day, Ethan waited for May, watching for any sign of her, hoping every morning when he woke that she would have reappeared as mysteriously as she had disappeared; but day after day there was no sign of her.

'Look at him, Tucker,' Martha said one day. 'He's hardly eating, and he doesn't show interest in much. I just don't know what to do for him anymore.'

'I only wish I knew where May was. I would go and fetch her myself,' Tucker told Martha.

As the weeks turned into months, Tucker and the rest of his family left Tattlebury, saying they would probably be back the following year. As Martha had promised Tucker, they bought him a new wagon and gave him some money for all his help around the place in the past months.

The departure of Tucker and his family left a huge hole in the daily life at Tattlebury. Martha and Ethan had grown used to having them around and this only served to push Ethan into a worse state of depression.

Then one day Martha couldn't find Ethan around. She searched high and low, but couldn't find him anywhere. Some while later, she was standing at the kitchen sink doing her washing up when she heard the sound of a lorry engine. Looking out of the kitchen window, she saw a lorry pull into the yard. As it drove closer, she saw who the driver was.

She ran out into the yard. 'Oh God, Ethan, what on earth are you doing?' she said to herself.

Ethan came closer but, not braking in time, he went crashing through the big fence and out into the field. Then the door of the lorry fell open and Ethan stumbled out.

'What are you doing?' Martha shrieked.

'I'm learning to drive a lorry, Aunt Martha. Then I'm going to get myself a new trailer, and I shall be off to find May. But I won't leave Tattlebury until the work is done.'

Martha looked worried.

'You have to understand, I've waited for May long enough. I have to find her. I don't feel there is much to hold me here anymore. I just have to go.'

'I understand,' Martha answered, and she smiled as Ethan put his arm around her slim shoulders. 'But look what you've done to your lorry!'

'Don't worry, the damage is minor, and I'll sort it out later. Right now I'm hungry,' he said, leading her back to the house. Martha felt the familiar feeling of love, and thanked God for whatever chance had brought Ethan to her.

⁂ ⁂ ⁂

At Longdrive Manor, Charlotte sat up in bed, staring fixedly ahead of her.

'Charlotte, you have to understand, there was nothing we could do,' her mother was saying.

It was early in May, and Charlotte had given birth prematurely to a baby girl. Within a few moments of beginning her life, the baby had died.

'But I heard the baby crying, Mother, I heard her!'

'Charlotte, you did not. It was your imagination. Believe me, I know how the mind plays tricks. You hear what you want to hear. I'm sorry that I could not do anything.'

Charlotte began to sob. 'All that pain for nothing. . .'

'Now, Charlotte,' said her mother comforting her, 'try not to upset yourself; you must get some rest. Lie down and try to sleep.'

Her mother left the room, and went to find her husband. She found him in the servant's quarters.

'We'll arrange a christening and funeral,' said Squire Weatherfield, looking at the still form of his granddaughter. 'But I'll have the time of my life with *him*,' he said picking up his tiny grandson. 'The son I never had! At last I get my revenge on the Gypsies.

'I can't let you do this,' his wife replied.

'You have no choice,' he retorted. 'I am going to send Charlotte away and keep him.' He held his grandson in his arms.

Outside the door, Mr and Mrs Foot, two of the house servants, were listening. They had worked for the Squire nearly all their lives. But finding out what a twisted and evil man he was, they could stand by and watch no longer.

'We can't let him do that! I'm going to find out who the father is, and tell him,' said Mrs Foot.

'But you'll get the sack!' said her worried husband.

'I'm resigning,' his wife replied.

Mr Foot did not agree with her, but he knew not to argue.

✳ ✳ ✳

Over the following months Ethan learned to drive and passed his test. He bought a Willoughby trailer to pull behind his motor, and when the work was finished at Tattlebury he decided to prepare for his journey. The year was fast running out. It was October when Ethan finally left Tattlebury. He knew that he was breaking Martha's heart, but he had to find May. He had to make her understand that he was truly sorry for what he had done.

Martha was indeed very lonely, but she knew that one day there would be a knock on the door, and Ethan would be back. She waited while the leaves fell from the trees and she looked out across the ploughed fields and windswept woodlands.

One day, Martha did indeed hear a knock on the door. She ran to answer it, but standing outside was an elderly woman.

'Excuse me,' she said, 'we're looking for Ethan Bray.'

'I'm sorry,' said Martha, 'Ethan's not here, he left some time ago.'

'Then may I have a word with you?' she beckoned to an older man standing by the gate.

Martha invited both of them in. 'What can I do for you,' she asked.

'We used to work at Longdrive Manor. We have something to tell you.'

'If you've come about the baby, Ethan and I know. It was a girl and she died.' Martha's voice was full of emotion.

'No, you don't understand, they were twins; one was a boy and one was a girl. The boy is still alive. He's five months old, he has big brown eyes and the makings of brown curly hair. He doesn't look at all like the Weatherfields.'

Martha's face showed shock. 'No, it can't be true. Ethan doesn't know,' she told them.

'It is true, Charlotte Weatherfield doesn't even know herself, because she went a little crazy after the baby died. She told everybody that she heard the baby cry so they sent her away to some sort of asylum. The Squire insisted that nobody told her about the boy.'

'Oh God!' Martha exclaimed. 'I must tell Ethan. I must find him. We must do something.'

✳ ✳ ✳

Ethan had been on the road for nearly two months without finding any sign of May. He was in Devon now and the weather had changed. It was December and it was snowing. Ethan pulled into a petrol station and stepped out of his lorry.

'You look like a real Romany,' said the man from the station.

'Yes, well that's what I am,' said Ethan. It was very cold, with flurries of snow and Ethan could see his breath in front of him. He stamped his feet.

'That's strange,' said the garage hand, 'two Romanies in two days. Only yesterday a Gypsy wagon passed here. There was a Gypsy girl with blonde hair holding the reins. She had a

116

young boy with her, as dark as they come. Romanies, make no mistake.'

Ethan went white as he turned to look at the man. 'Do you know where they went?' he asked urgently.

'Yes, they parked up in the woods on the other side of that house,' he said, pointing up the hill. 'I saw them when I went home.'

'Are they still there?'

'They were when I left this morning, and it's only nine now,' the man replied.

Ethan jumped into his lorry and soon caught sight of the wagon in the clearing of the woods. He could not see any sign of life. He imagined they would both be in bed. He parked along the roadside and walked back to the wagon. A thin veil of smoke was coming from the chimney. He walked up the slippery steps and gently pushed the open door a little further. Johnny was lying on the bottom bunk, and May was on the top one. They were both fast asleep.

Ethan bent down by the fire and threw some more wood into the flames. He thought about his past, about Martha and Jack. He thought about Tucker, coming into his life almost like a guardian. He thought about Martha's and Jack's goodness to him. He would always be thankful.

The sky was clearing as the breeze blew the snow clouds away. Ethan heard someone stir and he went over to the bunks. Wintry sunshine shed its pale light through the windows picking up the gold in May's fair hair, making her look almost like an angel. She stirred; she opened her eyes and closed them against the weak sunshine. Then, blinking again, she opened them.

'Ethan! What are you doing here?'

'I've been searching for you, May. I couldn't wait any longer. I still love you and I want to marry you, if you will have me.'

'I've been away long enough, Ethan,' she replied, 'and now I think it's time for you to take me home, back to Tattlebury. Let's go back to where we began.'

May reached out her hand, and Ethan kissed it gently. May's eyes gave him the answer he needed. He was her future, she was his and the life before them would answer so many questions.

'Let's go,' he said, 'we have a long journey back home.'